SCHILLING

from a study in lost time

A NOVEL BY TERRELL GUILLORY

A Pleasure Boat Studio Book

Guillory, Terrell
Schilling / Terrell Guillory
ISBN: 1-929355-09-2
First printing

Library of Congress Control Number: 2002114645

Design and composition by Lee Ryder

Published by Pleasure Boat Studio: A Literary Press
201 West 89th Street, #6F
New York, NY 10024
Tel/Fax: 888-810-5308
Email: pleasboat@nyc.rr.com
URL: http://www.pbstudio.com

For Angela

&

in memory of William Arrowsmith, long-time friend:

loyal, gifted, and humane

I O *It was a cold autumn dawn. In his sleep he reached for the covers before he realized it was morning, and then he awoke with that amazing awareness that sometimes takes the mind from sleep in an instant. The objects in the room were dim, the light less than colorful, still shadowy; the table, the Morris chair, the door, the closet and windows numb in their outlines, an aching impreciseness in every contrast. He reached for the covers again and moved his legs to where they had created the greatest warmth. For a moment he thought he was in bed at home and he was a child again; the moment passed. The next moment he found that he felt well, then he remembered that earlier he had risen and given himself a shot of morphine and gone back to sleep.*

He found his glasses on the table radio, then his watch, and saw that he had awakened an hour earlier than usual. Why, on this morning? There was no difference today that he could recall, there was nothing to happen, the barber wasn't coming, the doctor wasn't coming, there were no sudden new visitors, there was no place to go. No one stirred yet in the house. It was the hour of the morning when only cooks open screen doors and quietly begin the day. Not even the sound of wood burning, or an odor of bacon. When had he last heard wood burning in a cook stove, a roaring in the flues, iron plates shifted on the stove top with a cast iron key, every shift changing the sound of the fire? Fire. A word he pronounced as "fayah." Had the fire been lit on the gas range; was the cook in the kitchen? He heard nothing.

It was cold. He rubbed his feet together, the dead skin of sixty-odd years of shoe-wearing, scratchy and sounding like paper and permitting little warmth. He wiggled his toes into a crevice of the covers and curled them; still no warmth. He thought of getting up for another blanket but he was afraid to spill the well-being he felt, and in that moment genuine light struck the windowsill and he watched it crawl into the room, across the floor and up a wall. He heard birds, faintly at first, then in greater numbers. Had they been singing all the time? He listened then for a rooster crow and thought he heard one far in the distance. Somewhere there was a bell: a switch engine stopped in the rail yards. The night before he remembered the sound of a train passing through; when was that? He listened for the creak of a board and heard none.

In the corner of the room the light had struck an aspidistra. He remembered MacFarland's rubber plant standing in the corner of the classroom, the Scot with his drunken brogue of Highland tuning talking of anatomy and life, endlessly talking a music no one could ignore of how it was his task to make doctors out of men and that meant there wasn't much to work with. He remembered the music, and the morality and the anatomy had become stored in his nervous system. No one had influenced him more. And the Scot had lain in a seeping grave for forty years.

The plant was a shape of voiceless life, aloof intelligence, in this instant growing, somehow decisions being made. An amazing thing, an amazing shape, an amazing idea of form and system and intent. What intent? To be.

Grave, like departures of boats, or slow beginning rain in empty streets, the true sun struck the plant and cast a shadow against the wall. The plant seemed happy, which he knew was wrong, but he had accepted the loneliness of humans and the habit of attributing emotions to dumb objects in the absence of communication with any intelligence but his own. Grave and inexorable, the sun.

The war was over, but so recently it could not yet be realized. Yet his son had not come home. He had landed in San Francisco in August and gone directly to school in California. He hadn't written, though he *had called once in late August and the doctor had heard only once since. The doctor had wanted him to come: he wanted to hear about the war, where he had been, what he had seen. Rationalizations. He wanted to see the boy. They were unlike. Each thought the other strange, Dr. Schilling supposed. Nevertheless....*

His last child, the other three dead, was an agony to him. Ineluctable, opaque, distant, though he knew the boy to be exceptional in intelligence with a cast of mind he had sympathized with in his own thought. How many hours has a man thought? How many sympathies have gone unexpressed? How many lives has he looked into, saying nothing. The boy was like the others, the actual and the possible of his inner life, thought of for hours, yet scarcely saluted, sometimes never met, often only suspected, usually only conjectured. A woman with a peach pit caught in her throat, dying; a minister with his left shoulder drooping, obviously once broken. The issue of thought is nothing; it is used to justify the little action a man takes in his life, and the rest of it melts away like dreams as though it had never been. The sobs and the terror, unrecorded and transient and forgotten, yet coming again. Life is an unwritten record lived in the mind as though dreamed, alone, knowing it is alone, goes nowhere, begins nowhere, is as instantaneous as thought and as lost as afterthought, justified if at all by the exhortation, To be.

The sun was quite vivid, its reflection on a piece of metal bright and harsh. The numbness had left the room and it was warmer. He wiggled his toes and heard the creak of a board. He heard the ring of a skillet struck against the sink in the kitchen; someone moving in the shuffle of slippers.

He put his arms akimbo under his head and looked at the ceiling, a two-inch planking painted gray with crevices, a string of cobweb moving slightly directly above him. By what wind? Perhaps by the rising heat of his body. Could that be? Gone. The thought was gone. Gone. He was back again thinking which should bend to which, thought to action, action to thought? Which is better, thought unrecorded, uncast in action, or action unbending to thought as though thought had never existed? There was an issue, an egress into a solid controversy as old as intelligence. He knew better, and did nothing; or not enough. And he acted and regretted. Insoluble, the problem of acting intelligence. Nothing. No; torn. Failed. The cobweb moved from currents in the room, hot and warm transfers from object to object of differing native temperatures. Perhaps. Yet it moved. Failed.

Mary would come to the room at any moment. His sister-in-law would stand in the doorway and lean against the facing and yawn quietly and speak to him about how he had passed the night. He hated to move his bowed arms from beneath his head. The morning had begun with peace, seldom and true peace. There was no pain, except the reluctance to move about, a sense of limitation. On the table near the wall which the sun had not struck was the hotplate and guinea-colored boiler, the needles, cotton, syringes and morphine.

Some of his thought had sung of his life, and how many hours had he given to that? Most of it was as elusive as recollection of one's first rain on a roof while going to sleep. Moments came back to him as unruly as kaleidoscopic images. But his life could be summed up with three fifths of his hand. The rest was conversation, random and repetitive, seldom obviously relevant. Moments, smelled in the present, inchoate sensing and the following pursuit, the baying after origins, initiations, practice, returns. The blind capture of some beginning or some turning, insignificant and abortive: the first time he had seen coal led him nowhere but to amusement and nostalgia, a sense that he was alive. But moments with no scent to begin with, insignificant to the senses, led to instances, actions and flaws he could count with three

*fifths of his hand, and on this tripod his life crawled into its con-
cluding seconds.*

II

O The oysters. Vermilion Bay, green; the sand,
fleshly tan, went curving unduned, broken by thatches of plants
and empty fires unlit since summer. Burnished by the wind they
all went there when they were alive, the brothers; Anna; Quero.
The water of the gulf, then unpopulated by great steamers, might
be imagined through Southwest Pass, beyond Tigre Point; with no
odor of true sea wind, no rise of boat smoke, heraldic and exciting,
they might have been inland on a green lake, sultry and tidal. If it
had not been for the oysters.

Charcoal and green, shards of dead fires haunting, half buried
in the sand, lonely tokens of humanity and life. Clumps of grass
like faggots bundled, bent from the coast wind, dead and senseless,
the sand, the water, clouds in the sky. Trees. Inland, a copse
turning, one dead gum tree alone festooning moss, the air
autumnal, desolate, presage of November cutting the salted air.
They went there from the rice-prairie country of a Sunday to feast
from hampers heavy as bricks, to remain until twilight drove them
to Abbeville and John's home arriving in the dark, kerosene lights
in the windows, the milking long done, some cattle disturbed
when the buggy drew up. The five brothers went there to walk
barefoot in the sand, Abe to fish, Tom to study the horizon, the
other three to talk about crops and business and the affairs of the
world; or to join the women to sing "Green Grow the Laurels" and
"Sweet Betsy from Pike" and notice the birds on their southern

flight alight briefly on Marsh Island; alight and whirr upward again in precise, startled, squadron flight to fly farther, perhaps over the naked open gulf; or the tide come in, embayed and indolent. To toe shards of glass and burnt wood from the sand, as though the day would never end, the women unburdening the hampers while talking of last week, calling far down the beach to come on to dinner, time to eat, Anna, Quero, John's wife and Mary, when they were all young. A crane had been in his vision for a time before his mind focused upon it. He sat alone, apart from his garrulous brothers, Abe fishing far down the beach, his cigar smoke blown like a banner, the women spreading the food away from the tide, where the marsh grass began. He was thinking of the oysters bedded against a sand spit, a wallow for mollusks made by the sea. He thought of them submerged from the wind, palpitant with the tide, encased in their adamant vesicles. Even now they were dying, not merely the old but the fresh spat that the waves had never tempered, rocked as time rocks clocks and men. Dying. And they were dying a hundred years before they were born, and they were dying in all the centuries before they existed, before this bay settled here during its last recession from the prairie; and they were dying before they took form as oysters, before they were heirs of another death, a vanished form of pulsation perhaps from deeper seas; dying. Hidden and breathing, without conscience, they held almost vaginally some gift, some secret, some object or state sought and forever unattainable. They brooked no intrusion but the occasional sand and bits of water life, perfume of the sea. He thought of them as warm, febrile beneath the tide and sun, rocked in darkness under the sea-moon; febrile and glistening from unseen glands, rudimentary and pristine, sexual, yet unlike his realization of sexuality the perspiring aggression upon a prone flesh, breathless and violent; they were tempered and patient, unlike the mobile flesh men encountered in their experience, special and unkind, tainted by its very privacy; they were certain, unlike the uncertainty he tolerated, a burden, a trouble in his mind. Apart. Silent. Already dying.

He would never have noticed the crane had it not hung over the water at one edge of the bay, refusing to alight. White, suspended bird, trees, waters, clouds and sky, held still for a moment; for the time it takes a mind to turn loose its interior images and admit others, become aware that life is a motion, that voices have not truly stopped. The crane, certainly in motion though scarcely, taunted him by its seeming sharp hanging in air, legs furled. He remembered that a crane had hung in the blue air in the same way the week before through the courtroom window while the legal voices droned on in French, he, the doctor, perspiring from the last hot day of October, trying to be attentive.

IT WAS A NIGHT that would have shaken the Middle Ages, hounded the peasant out of his dreams along the Norman coast: woody lightning in the Rhine Valley shuddering in the minds of sleepless souls on the edge of forests, fixing murderers in shimmering electricity, Teuton blood veined in error, horses by trees neighing by thunder in the woods in the sepulcher of night. A lost knight asleep on his horse in the woods of Lorraine, bark shining in the horrible light, his *hauberk* like the fur of some monster, blue in the light and rain, alone, asleep, his horse bent, white eyes open in the thunder; terror alone in the woods, coming from somewhere, going somewhere not knowing where in this course from hot seas and lost beaches through wooded continents as man. The old horsemen muscled in glory, jostled by panic, lathered in dead souls, anointed with serum, gall and bowels, convicted in slaughter, trembling in trees by a blue horse's haunch, night in the woods lit by a tic in the eye of God, horses unferruled in the molecular trace.

THE FRENCH KINGS ARE DEAD, their faces gracing cornices in dead halls of Europe; their wives are dead, faces staring beside them; their servants are dead; the cocks that crew are dead. Their minds are dead, its continents are dead, its tribes of barbaric mixtures are dead, what once was etched in the acid of terror on their brains is gone, the old pains and motives are gone: all dead. Then why?

He rode through a lateral rain, his horse shying from the lightning, his glasses half off so he could see in the darkness, his poncho dinning noisily from the tattoo of the rain. Leather too wet for creaking, the slop of hooves in the mud, the wind inside his hood burning his ears, it took him an hour to get there and he didn't know why he had been called, what waited for him; to a tavern late at night.

Ardoin was dead when he arrived, still sitting at his wine. The cakes, sprinkled with white powder, half eaten from an oil-cloth pouch, were still sitting at his elbow where they had replaced him after drawing him up from the floor where he had lain in his green vomit; not yet rigid though it had been more than an hour. The bartender was sitting on a stool, a man named Percell; late-drinking farmers sat at one table while the drunkards of the village sat at another, watching the doctor make no inquiry, only examining the mouth and tongue, feeling the stomach, looking at the nails.

The bartender silently handed Schilling a glass of wine, but after taking it, the doctor shook his head and handed it back.

There, the bartender said, motioning toward the cakes. The doctor picked them up, smelled them, then tasted one with his tongue, spitting lightly, asking for the wine. He spit the first mouthful of wine on the sawdust floor; the drunkards laughed loudly, the farmers silently. The doctor smiled and said in French (it is all in French), It's not good for you.

He took another sip of the wine and asked the bartender if Ardoin had had convulsions, how long he had taken to die; why wasn't he called sooner?

Could you have saved him? the bartender asked.

No, he shook his head.

He asked for two men. Three men moved; the third he sent for the deputy. Two round tables were drawn together. Ardoin was placed on them, his knees relaxed, dangling from the second, his wrists relaxed, a cameo ring studded in pitted gold against the checkered cloth. A deer with bulbous eyes and six points hung half-necked over a mirror, a stain of blood the color of syrup still across his windpipe. The sawdust on the floor had lost its odor; the windows were barred against the rain; outside wooden doors folded to protect the glass. Black lanterns hung from the rafters, their chimneys sooty; on every third table a lamp sat, their chimneys cleaner but the light flickering from untrimmed wicks. The bartender chewed tobacco and leaned over to drop a string of brown into a spittoon, saying nothing. The doctor undid the coat and shirt, ran his fingers over the hollow of the sternum, hair spreading from the chest toward the arms and the stomach, black and violent. He saw passion marks on the shoulders and throat from teeth and suctions two days old.

The deputy came and after a glass of wine and questions, borrowed a wagon to take Ardoin to the doctor's office where he would lie until morning. On the way home the rain had quieted so that, in spite of the horse's breathing and the suck of the mud, he could hear the "creee…" of a coon in a pecan tree, a sound that had terrified him in his youth riding home from a *faydedo* before those woods became plains of rice and cotton. At his back step the thunder rolled up from the south, the Gulf, vibrating in the great dinner bell that hung at the right of the porch, a hood of bronze taken from a locomotive in a sawmill town.

THE COURT DRONED ON. A hovering of gnats stood by the mimosa outside the courtroom window. He thought of the prosecutor's liver; he thought of the judge's prostate, the heavy man sitting now with a string tie and a straw fan behind a mahogany desk draped with a flag held by a book, bible, rock and inkwell. Eustacia Ardoin sat, blonde and plain, yet sexual and youthful, where the Napoleonic Code had her sit, arraigned and single: the village already too large to be totally interested in her trial and death, the courtroom not quite full, the fall day cracked by the shrillness of children on the school ground three blocks away, breaking not a cold of October, but a stillness. The silence further broken by wagons and horses squeaking and snorting in rutted streets, or the unkind call of a grocer to his helper, poor prisoner of produce and sex and rural roads. Or a Negro would drive slowly through the street, never hitting the caked mud along the rut, an un-repaired wheel striking wood with the sound of *hing, hing, hing,* slowly, tediously, until it had passed through the village. The gnats made no noise unless a mosquito joined them. The court droned on and the shadow of a mimosa struck the back of a merchant on the jury, the shadow rising and falling as the man breathed.

Eustacia Ardoin, twenty-six, blonde, odd, the daughter of rice growers and pecan harvesters from west of Mamou; a good family, Eustacia neither the youngest nor the oldest, but somewhere in the middle, married at twenty to a man who was both a farmer and drunkard and a traveler and wanderer, not back toward the French of New Orleans but west through Texas into Mexico and California. Forever ruined. A fisherman at times, a hand treated with the fishhook still in it after two days of finishing his work and traveling from the Gulf, the odor of fish, sea and pus about him; smiling while the doctor took the hook out, Eustacia perhaps pregnant six months ago, spreading herself on his table, her vagina straw, red and vulnerable before him, her state innatal. A passionate woman, her body not merely frightened, but also wise, instinctively sniffing through the clinicism, waiting with the repose and will of a patient woman, enduring and supine.

Crushed sugar cane piled bonily in a field, burning and smoking next to a sawmill spur, wind carrying sparks away from railroad ties stacked for another spur never built, the odor of creosote, smoke and autumn. He had been called out of the courtroom, the court adjourning at his leaving, riding the bay because the chestnut was ill-shod, following the manured path along the railroad beds not long from suppertime. A dinner bell sounded from the village through the woods two miles straight across the fields where the Negroes were quitting, some already walking lanes toward big houses carrying empty pails for backdoor food, or milk paid for milking that had been stored during the heat of the day in a field-well. Marci M'sieur, one of three Negro boys said when he held up his horse to let them step up out of a marsh and take the trail with a string of bass and a broken pole, talking Louisiana French, a remnant of Europe dissonant in their mouths. *Boo-coo poisson*, one said, then all laughed and passed on, the doctor riding on, the shadow of his horse falling down the high railroad trail into the willows and the darkening marsh already singing with night.

An Irish Paddie had wandered out of the east, freighting it, until he had taken a series of wrong turns and wound up near Mamou with dysentery from eating fly-blown fruit. The doctor had sent him down the spur to the sawmill where now he worked and stood eel-faced and silent beside the man with a crushed hand, clipboards of invoices hanging on the wall, all that remained of management except for the watchman this near suppertime. A silent man, there had been an immediate bond between them, a spring that in neither of them had ever come to the surface. The Irishman, Michelo the Negroes called him, thinking him Spanish, spoke only English with a brogue that was more foreign than Spanish, an accent that could be understood only by the doctor and one other man in Mamou, a Welsh merchant also out of the northeast; a wanderer from Virginia, or some port gained with a blind fare paid for passage to America in 1886 from Liverpool, afterward wandering. Michelo had tics of speech when he bothered to speak. *Roo roo roo*, he would say, and nothing more, its meaning plain. In late hours when even the fireflies slept and the porch was deserted, the boarders having gone in because of the mosquitoes, he would sit with the doctor saying nothing.

There was little to be done for the hand; it had been crushed between two logs. He gave the man a clumsy opiate and cleaned the blood away and told him to spend the night on the manager's cot. The Paddie was the watchman, but tonight he was off. He rode back to town with the doctor on back of the bay.

On this night he was talkative.

I worked far a man who owned a bay horse.

Where was that?

Tullamoor. I was a blacksmith's boy wantin' a bay harse.

When was that?

Twenty yaers ago. The things ye want and niver have.

What else did you want?

I wanted me a pretty red-headed woman. I used to say if iver I had me a pretty red-headed woman and a bay harse, I'd build me a corral for the harse and ride the woman. Now I'd build me a corral for the woman and ride the harse.

And that was all he said except for humming, *roo roo roo*. A plate of chicken awaited them after dark, the Paddie boarding in the same house from the time the doctor had befriended him, his room below those of the doctor and his wife, an awareness of vagrant intelligence coming through the floor, the doctor, before sleeping, sometimes looking down in the dark through the floor wondering what he was thinking: submission to fatality.

He knew the moment the Paddie changed his position in the porch chair after the last boarder had gone in, his wife already asleep since supper, a clear but slowly weathering night; he knew before the Paddie said anything. What amazed him was not the thought, the realization; but rather the Paddie's generosity to speak, to go to that trouble. Yet he did not know at that moment who it was: it had never occurred to him. He had been afraid of it, as every man is; and like all intelligent men he had prepared himself to accept it as he had prepared himself to accept death and disaster, like the flood on the day of his wedding. He was even grateful that adultery was not true disaster; but even then he was blaming himself. He could not bring himself to ask questions not only because it was beneath him, or because he had accepted it as a possibility but because he had already thought of himself as being to blame, exactly as one feels to blame for the continual cruelty transpiring daily on another continent, as in the name of the human race one accepts guilt, he accepted guilt in the name of men confronted with great beauty fool enough to expect it to be benignant, true and good: an error, a blending of parts forever separate.

The Paddie said, Yere're right, what yere're thinking. Ye saw that this afternoon, didn't ye?

Who is it?

I wouldn't have mentioned it if it hadn't been who it is. The fireflies have settled in quiet bushes; there is no moon. In a year he will own this house, the mimosa tree will still stand outside the porch through which the moon will rise, but the vegetables will be transplanted and in their place azaleas will grow. In six months his first child will die on the day of its birth.

Who is it?

That fellow Ardoin.

What?!

He was here everyday for three months after the spring fishing on the Gulf. I was here, sleepin'.

It had never occurred to him. Eustacia had killed her husband because he was a brute. But of course: she had killed him because he was a brute.

His wife knew. I hae seen her walk past in the mid-morning when the house was quiet, the servants gone, after that fellow would come in the back door, and go upstairs with somebody.

Are you sure?

I hae repaid yer favors, Doctor. I'll be wanderin' soon. Again he was silent until he began humming just before he went in for the night, *roo roo roo.*

The doctor sat alone for an hour, until the fireflies were blown out of a bush by a freshet of wind, the odor of rain sudden and cool. The oil wells were not yet pumping over the prairies of Mamou, Mamou not all prairies and rice and sugarcane, only beginning, seeming to begin. He sat alone for an hour after the rain began, gustily at first, then settling into a sleepy falling, the fireflies gone beyond the yard, the business houses square and dark, the court, its aspiration truncated and unfinished. He knew...before he went in and climbed the stairs.

The court began as it had begun the day before, as though there had been no interruption. The prosecution ended its indictment, its case. The defense called its first witness.

Insane, he said, and answered questions, short and of no consequence. They sent her to the asylum in Alexandria, Eustacia turning to look at him when they led her from the courtroom. In his mind the image of her blond vagina, pink and hungry, gnawer of flesh. The court adjourned.

ABBEVILLE AGAIN, and full autumn, dead vines, the August plants no more than stalks bent or fallen to the rain, hieroglyphs of summer. October is gone and the time has fallen into that pulsant quiet between the first and second cold spells not Indian Summer, but the inhalation after the first hiss of winter. The hogs were slaughtered on the first frosty morning, the steam of their butchered flesh rising, their blood running into the rimey grass sparkling with pretty crystals. Now the meat hangs on hooks in the smokehouse, crocks of salted bacon stacked like Egyptian urns in the corner of a tomb. Someone was always coming; the ham dwindled first; but there would be another killing in December, and by spring there would still be a half dozen hams glazed with salt and mold. A wind had blown the lattice of the porch from its pegs; it would not be replaced until after the April winds; it leaned against the side of the house. Lawn seats had been taken in; certain plants had been taken up to be stored in the house; bulbs in the barn; potatoes in a storm cellar underneath the house; the canning stood in the pantry from floor to ceiling.

Someone was always coming. He had walked out under an oak tree and was toeing a child's toy half buried in the sand when he heard the horse and buggy. They were neighbors. As John came out to greet them, the doctor had already turned the corner of the house toward the barn. He loved this place; he had been born here behind these oaks, playing under them in the sand, and coming here was a token of peace regardless of who was dead, the long dyings already begun, that chain drawn through a man's life with links hammered out of mortality no matter how occasional and far apart, so that sometime he must follow it back link by link, death by death to whoever was first. Life is a chain of dead faces remembered binding humans to eternal pain. Too painful to remember except in silence, not in that unhoned ax of talk country people wield on Sunday afternoons. He saddled the black mare he had given John, the horse he had driven the day he met his wife. He led the horse quietly to the edge of the fields, mounted and cut across grass toward the Gulf.

Eustacia Ardoin, blonde, eccentric, lost, but surely not insane. He thought of the nights he had lain beside his inert wife, their marriage not consummated for a year, his desire rising, thinking of Eustacia alone, Ardoin at the Gulf. Lying in a country town, his thought opening tomb on tomb before sleep, he would think of her in her strangeness, no one coming. Called feeble-minded by loose felons of the spirit, people of peasant anger, they tightened the knot on her life. He lay homeless before sleep watching her pace, her house the only light in town except for the tavern. When he would go on a call and pass her house at midnight, he had the sense that they were the only two minds awake in the prairie night. Nothing but the stars and minds separated forever.

For a time his horse walked brisket high in grass bent north from onshore winds. On the horse that day he never believed she had killed Ardoin because of any fineness of her thought, but because of a final degree of insult.

RAGING IN THE WOODS of herself, hearing the syrinx and the winds blowing her nothing, she would dance ballet in her living room all afternoon. She would play some passage on her piano, remember it, hum and dance; play another passage, remember that and dance until she was exhausted and happy.

Carelessly, she left the curtains open so she could be seen from the street, and one afternoon while she was roosting breathlessly on the arm of the sofa after a half hour of her woods and hills, a knock came at the door. Wiping her perspiration on her sleeve, wrapping her long loosed hair in a quick knot with a pin to hold it, she went to the door and looked through the single pane of glass. No one was there. She raised herself on tiptoe and looked down and around; no one was there. Finally she opened the door and on the step there was a large potted azalea in full bloom.

She picked it up and admired it, turning it in the late sunlight. A stick was stuck in the dirt, a note wrapped around it. Smiling, delighted, puzzled, she set the pot on the porch banister and unwrapped the note. The street was empty, the ebb tide of a village at supper. The note read, We're praying for you. Unsigned.

The story went around until the time of the trial the following year, of how Crazy Eustacia walked up to the preacher's house while the reverend's wife was serving his supper, knocked on the door, and when the reverend's wife came, Eustacia dropped the pot and plant at the holy feet, ball of dirt and pot exploding over the clean front porch, then walked away without a word, humming an uncouth passage from pagan music, dancing a step or two when she reached the gate, to fly down the sidewalk like one demented, skipping, arms flaring in the indignity of a step to the music of Debussy.

There were other stories, all leading to the image of feeble-mindedness, harmless dementia. Except to the preacher's wife and the other church ladies, she was an object of humor and ridicule behind her back. The good church sisters found no humor in her before or after the incident of the potted azalea. How people who go to bed at eight can keep such sentry is a mystery, but it was generally known to the ladies that Eustacia was abroad after dark many nights of the year, even in the rain, walking the streets of Mamou with a shawl over her head, sometimes her face bared to the rain in sheer promiscuous sensuality. No one ever mentioned witch until Ardoin's murder, but whore was common.

Others who saw her when she took her walks, perhaps once a week in warm weather, perhaps once or twice when the rain was gentle in the spring and summer, men who drank until late, neither mocked nor accosted her. They knew her father, her family; and they had worked and drunk with Ardoin. Some of them might joke about her in the daylight; but in the evening they would tip their hats when they saw her abroad, and they would move off the sidewalk in deference to her passing, and walk along thinking she was kin to them in some way, nightwanderers, night-waiters, nightlost.

She had beauty, but not in the structure of her face. It was the tone of her face, a liveliness both gentle and alert; an expression of vital thoughts beneath which structure lay comely.

She made no pronouncement of her sexuality; the clothes she wore were poorly chosen and of eccentric colors. She had no poise in daylight but walked flat-footed with a jog to her flesh like a field girl, but at night she was like a daughter of the month of June, walking barefoot in the sandy sidewalk, sometimes her shawl trailing behind her like a train. She was always alone, dying inside while her heart beat out unspeakable passions.

Ardoin loved her but considered her better than he. He was never at home, and when he came to Mamou from shrimping on the gulf or cutting trees around Kinder or Opelousas, he tried to show her that he loved her by listening to her dreams until he fell asleep. To Ardoin she was a child, and Ardoin was a wanderer who loved whores better than virgins, hilarity always, sobriety as a duty. He had married her because they were both escaping, he from a sense of shortened possibility, the vicious certitude of brute labor as long as he lived though he was a skillful man. Not a dreamer but an escapist, not even daring to dream, ever, from childhood. Drinking and fishing with friends, not even women unless he was alone and very drunk. His reputation among the reverent was that of a whoremonger; among the irreverent, that of a hard man in a fight and a good man to drink with.

On days when he was home, Eustacia played the violin, notes she had memorized from piano music of Debussy. He would lie listening to her, his bare feet on the arm of the divan, a long red-faced Frenchman in his late twenties, his eyes closed, the music exquisite to him, making him think of waves and coasts, quiet water and woods; a fish biting. When he came on weekends he would tell tales of the Ghost of the Calcasieu, lies Eustacia dismissed. To interest her he would lighten the lie to a myth of a crazy old man who lived along the Calcasieu whom no one ever saw but who stole all the fish of all the fishermen while they slept along the banks. Then, skipping legend, he would say there were old men who lived in the cattails along the banks, tying untended lines to fallen slender branches, long switches whipping when bass or catfish struck. Then making legend by lying a little, he told how the bargemen would get their suppers by going close to the bank and cutting the lines the vanished old men had tied, fish drowned at the end of them. She was as tolerant of his fantasy as he was of hers and never challenged him.

Where are we going to ever go, Ardoin? she would ask.

New Orleans, he would say.

When?

Someday soon.

The next time you come?

Maybe.

I want to go somewhere. Can we go to St. Louis after we go to New Orleans?

Maybe.

When? When?

Soon. Soon.

I don't want any clothes, I don't want to spend any money, I just want to see everything, everything before I die. Can we begin soon?

Soon.

Very soon?

Sleep, Stacia.

Shall we go somewhere today? They're in church.

Sleep, Stacia.

Maybe if we left right now we could be in New Orleans by tomorrow.

Soon. Sleep, Stacia.

Maybe in the fall?

In the fall. Sleep, Stacia. Sleep. Sleep.

CLUMPS OF SEDGE GREW in the less worn parts of the road, and the grasses grew higher as he passed through marshes and the odor of rot. When the rot was passed, he smelled the salt air. The horse was walking with a spring-footed puffing of sand from the frog of his foot; certain birds lighting on hidden estuaries, leaving again. Finally he reached the beach. He dismounted and led the horse into the fall's warm afternoon sand.

He had always thought considerably from youth, and that tinkering introspection of other people was, with him, a sustained open country, a plain of cities, or a wood. Or simple space with nothing. There were times when he thought through briars of motives, the unutterable complexity of human possibility, but he could not think of Eustacia Ardoin in this way. He thought of her on a plain, treeless and high, and in the silence of his mind felt his love for her never felt before unless curiosity is love.

There were three women in his life, Anna, Quero, and Eustacia Ardoin. Anna, his sister, he had loved, worshiped when he was in that groin anger of youth. Quero he had worshiped and married. Only Eustacia had set him free, had the spirit to accompany his imagination on its journeys. In that moment on the beach at Vermilion Bay in November of 1909, leading the black horse through the sand, he saw what it was to love her, that he had to love her, that something had to set him free. That his mind was not enough, that he couldn't love its images forever, that he must conceive of another companion. The archaeology of thought is sanded cities, buried lives and pasts, deserts of the dead where even the bay of a jackal is more important than civilizations of phantoms no matter how ideal and lost. His mind went alone with him, peopling great distances. He led the horse through a clump of gnats, swatting his face, the gnats stationary in the air as he walked on. The harmless quotidian distracted him for a moment; he thought of something else. He walked on in the sand toward the embayed nursery of mollusks, Ostreidae and men, leading the horse, black hide, reins and figure, alone. Twenty-five years pass.

III

O *How cold it is. When will he come on? He's so slow. It's a norther. Maybe Webber will come; maybe he's missed Webber. Why don't I have keys to the car? Did I ever have them? Never. He's never given me keys to the car. I told him I would be here at nine; it's nine now. Oh how the buildings rise, the light, the great beautiful light rising. Like a halo. Like the star of Bethlehem. How long is it till Christmas? Two months. I want Webber to have a suede jacket; he must buy Webber a suede jacket. The other boy's asleep on his feet, sitting on the running board. Back to Kemp, when he comes. I have missed seeing things for being in Kemp all my life. What could ever possess him to stay in these urchin towns? Big frog in a little pond. He makes me so nervous, lumbering and fat, that walk of his. What's he doing? The boy's cold. Put the fur around him. There. Mrs. Reasoner will like the remnants I bought. My only friend. The only true friend I've ever had. Where is he? He'll take his time and leave me sitting here. Then he'll drive back to Kemp, never talking to me.*

Then he'll want to mess around and I'm tired and disgusted and he can't do any good anyway. I live for Webber. I'm going to take him out of Kemp to Waco where he'll have a chance to make something of himself. There he is, coming down the street. Hurry up, fool.

I LOVE YOU, WEBBER, smiling with your collar up against the wind. I've bought you a new overcoat I want to give you before Christmas, I must give you before Christmas if I can afford to get you something else for Christmas. The overcoat is more important. I must give it to you on the first cold morning before you go to school. I love your face. You're so unlike Quero; could she really be your mother? Your teeth will be straight now; we've gone a year, only two years to go. I wish I could talk to you. But I've never been able to talk to anyone. I want to tell you how hard it's been, and not to make my mistakes. We're in a depression, and I have no money, and my patients have no money yet I have to work harder than before because they have no money and they need a doctor. I wish I could tell you what has meaning, but I've never been able to do that with anyone, and you're too young. It's a beautiful night. I hope she's at the car and she hasn't walked the boy to death today. I need an overcoat too. Did you know she's spent so much money I haven't been able to buy an overcoat for fifteen years? I see the parking lot. Two red lights and we'll be there.

I BEG YOUR PARDON...? Are you Dr. Thomas Schilling? Yes. The woman who stood beside them having approached from the street on which the traffic light shone green was in her late forties, attractively dressed. She had studied the man's profile from the time she crossed the street, the boy with him on his other side.

Dr. Schilling? From Mamou, Louisiana? I'm Eustacia Ardoin.

Now my name is MacIntyre. Dr. Thomas Schilling?

Yes. Yes.

Do you remember me?

Yes. Yes of course.

I knew it was you. I saw you from across the street. I'm going to meet my husband and my daughter. I live here in Dallas.

Eustacia Ardoin? I can't believe it.

Oh we lived in New York for a long time, my husband and I, after the war was over. Phillip is an engineer and his work takes him to South America. I'm going to meet my daughter who is taking ballet near the Medical Arts Building. Is this your son?

This is Webber.

I can't believe it.

I can't believe it either. Eustacia Ardoin, from Mamou?

Come see my daughter dance at the World's Fair next year. My husband's paintings have been on display in Dallas from time to time. I can't believe it either. You were such a kind man, Dr. Schilling. I remember you, riding down the street on a chestnut horse. Is that the color? Reddish brown? Oh, I remember you.

Eustacia Ardoin? When did you leave Louisiana? But she said nothing, and when she started to speak, the wind swallowed the words.

The light has changed, she said. He started to cross, looked back at her, put his foot back on the curb. She had her feet parted in leaving and remaining.

Come, she said. Come. And walked on, looking back. He crossed the street to catch the light. Seeing Quero waiting for him in the parking lot two blocks away at the end of the street, he hurried.

Eustacia Ardoin, neither duct nor princess: middle-aged fantasist leading a life a quarter century later in the streets of Dallas. Neither a route to freedom nor completion. How had she come this far? One Paddie on a firefly-serenaded porch had saved Eustacia's life, winds from the Gulf blowing her destiny at random. The Irishman had told among the last fireflies what became the index of summer. It was he who set Eustacia free. He lay in Arizona now, the fall Schilling met Eustacia on the streets of Dallas; had lain there for twenty years. Some sheriff had written the doctor in 1915 forwarding a knife made in Bristol, a wallet of photographs faded, a silk handkerchief with perhaps some semblance of a woman long dead in its turn, its weave, its color, its odor of imagination.

The clump of gnats stationary beyond which he rides, now mounting the horse, figure, horse, sea as one as time.

NAPKIN RINGS OF SEA-IVORY hunted from Nantucket; silver polished with the skin of the lizard from the Pyrenees; bone china that sang like crystal; yellow linen with old coffee stains impossible to erase; a silver tureen the color of sour earth; the odor of guinea from the kitchen wedded to the scent of filé; the rice, beef, gumbo gone; now the coffee. Anna pours boiling water over the grounds gently, the black hot flower crawling into every corner. They are talking. Some wind stirs the young rice; outside some wind across the prairie bends the young rice. John is telling of a horse he has bought; Anna pours the coffee.

Through the window it is evening, the Negroes walking past to the lane gate carrying shares of milk in lard pails, the lettering worn off. A pointer roams the yard, meets a setter, greets the setter; a separation in dog trot division, aimless and wide as before. John is talking of how Negro Paul's son handles the horse, an intelligent boy of fifteen. The ones left at the table sip the coffee from demitasse. Schilling can hear the claws of pigeons perching and squabbling on the roof. Anna signals for him to finish his coffee; they walk out through the kitchen, Quero beginning to tell of a horse her father once had, a roan with a star in its forehead.

Outside a Negro closes the pasture gate across the windless yard. The setter's tail is a flag in the pasture grass, the pointer ahead of him on some fantastic scent. There is wind in the grass, but the trees are still. It is a long-shadowed spring hour just short of May, as painted and still as an Indian Summer, green and violent colors transfixed in the silent terror of life. The equinox is gone, its gloom cast out, as shadows trail under clouds across the fields, leaving forever. The decay of the South is the odor of mildew, sheets, books, clothing sour-sweet. The rains have soured the loam, yet the weeds attack the fences and the rice grows in a morass of ten feet of ground damp. They take the lane, closing the gate behind them.

I been hoping to get to Mamou, Tom, but we never get away from here. I haven't seen you folks since when?

We were here last fall.

Just before cold weather; I remember. The little girl didn't have no chance at all, Tom?

No. She lived three hours.

It's a shame.

Yes.

You been wanting a child.

Yes.

They walked on silently for a time, the dogs roving ahead afield.

I can understand that, Anna said.

What?

You wanting a child so bad.

Well, why not?

Why do you want the child? You don't want the child for the child.

What are you talking about?

Forget it. You folks didn't write.

Quero didn't write?

Naw! She never writes.

What? She says she does.

Once in a while we'd get a note from her about geraniums. Are you beginning to regret?

What do you mean?

You were so crazy to marry Quero, I just couldn't believe it. You never went crazy for anything in your life, and then you went crazy for Quero.

I love her.

Aw Tom, that's not love, that's crazy things. Tell me what's the matter.

Nothing.

Now you listen to me. None of the Schillings ever cared much for honesty in dealing with themselves; they gave the honesty to the other fellow. I asked Papa once and he said it was because we been poor for fifty years, we haven't got time for niceties. I don't believe that; I don't think none of them care about honesty except for their reputations. There is another kind of honesty and you know about that kind better than any of us. Time is going; I'm forty, and you must be thirty-five. There ain't time for lies anymore.

He walked along thoughtfully for a moment, then said, You suddenly look up, don't you?

You suddenly look up. That's right. And oh I'm telling you it hits, it hits hard. Look at me: look at me: I'm an old woman just about. Never married. I've got nobody and nothing. Well so you look up. But are you happy, Tom? That's what I want to know.

He pulled a piece of grass, juicy with spring. Chewed it. No, he said, but I've never been happy.

Well, she said, that's you. That's right, you've never been happy. I don't know why, she said, but it's true. I've always known that. Ever since you were a little boy you always went off alone, and if you laughed, then it was really funny. I used to look at you when you were a little fellow, look into those sad brown eyes and think, my Lord, what kind of a person is this? To suffer so. And nobody can ever tell why. And you can't ever tell anybody that it's true. You've never complained. But nobody knows you like I do, Tom.

That's true.

You're the best of the Schillings. Even John can't say he's made of himself what you have.

Whoa now....

It's true. You're the only one since Grandad who ever did anything for anybody. Do you know that you have a reputation, even here in Abbeville, of being a good doctor?

I didn't know that.

It's true. People talk about you with some awe. All these folks are kin, and word travels. I can't tell you the respect people have for you. It's just....

I didn't know that, he said. He wasn't sure what it meant, but it made him nervous. The last thing, the last killing burden to his nature was notoriety of any kind.

I just want to know if you're reasonably happy.

Well, I'm content. You know I'm happy in my way.

Honest?

Sure.

Your marriage too?

He tossed the grass and reached for another. No. I guess not.

Aha! I knew that.

How?

We've never talked about it. You want to?

Some. Chewing the grass.

Well what's the matter?

I don't know. Some things aren't too obvious. Some things I can't talk about. Quero's a high-strung woman.

What do you mean?

You know, she's nervous.

Is she a good wife to you?

How do you mean?

Is she a wife?

Oh yes. That's all fine. He remembered that it was the first time he'd ever lied to Anna. But in that instant it wasn't a lie. He conceived that the whole matter was his fault, that he had been remiss, and the subject raised now was painful.

I know she's high-strung. But what's it like to live with her?

I think she's unhappy.

That makes you unhappy.

Of course.

Well…. You're not going to say anything, so I will. You know what's wrong?

What? He almost stopped in his tracks, then forced himself on.

Honest?

Honest.

Well, now I've known this for a long time, I could see it, I could hear it in what she said. And I know in another way. She don't like the French, Tom. She don't like southern Louisiana and Cajuns, she calls them.

I'm not Cajun, you're not Cajun. We're a mixture.

I know that, you know that; but does she know that?

Of course she knows that! Of course she knows that! He was angry.

I think she knows the facts, but I don't think she knows the truth. To her, you're Cajun, I'm Cajun, all of us are Cajun.

A little Cajun, maybe. I like Cajuns.

They been coming down here since some fool president—who was it, Jefferson?—bought this swamp from—who was it, Napoleon?—and looking down at the French people. It's the way of anybody who ever had anybody born in the British Isles. Now that's it, Tom. And she is from that stock and she knows it and she'll never forget it to the day she dies. It's bred in 'em. It's there. And she's like that, raised that way, if not by her daddy, then by the preacher, especially the preacher, or the man who owns the store. You married somebody who considers herself a white woman, and you will never, never be a white man! Now hear me!

He was furious, threw the grass as far as he could, kept his place.

You don't like that, do you? It's true.

It's too stupid to be true. He thought of the dead kings, the cornices bright with faces rubbed with rain. All the dead halls and prayers and battles and plagues, songs and sentiments, noble and past. That great bloody cauldron, web on web spun since Rome, and in the timeless silence before. In that instant, at that moment, he knew it would turn out to be nothing, this life, this haunted moment ghosted with thought. The clarity passed. He was again in the illusion of going somewhere, finally. Chewing grass.

It may be, he said. But I think of her as more intelligent than that. The loss of the baby was hard.

I'm sorry for Quero, as I'm sorry for you. My feeling for Quero is sorrow. I don't like her. You hear?

I hear. How long are you going to live with John?

I got no place to go. Listen to me. Don't you ever forget your folks go back in this country since the Spanish and it's on the French side. Your granddaddy with the Alsatian name came walking through here from New Orleans where he got off a boat with a Bible and a book of Greek poetry. He was a scholar and I always thought you'd be the one but there ain't much chance to eat and spout poetry at the same time. But your mama's folks were planters who lived a good life before and after the civil war. You know what lost that French money—the money was always on the French side—improvement lost it. There wasn't anybody to apply improvement even after it had been accepted. Scared niggers and mumbling Frenchmen who'd rather *pirogue* in the bayou than hear of anything new. Catfishing, coon-hunting lost that money and you know why? Your landowning ancestors wouldn't push nobody to try anything new; fed them anyway with middling work like chopping woods down, slopping hogs, nigger work. Northern Louisiana just outdid southern Louisiana with pure English calculation. But money ain't the measure; it's what money can do that tells the inches. With money you might have gone east to school, or even to France. Your grandfather thought you were going to be a scholar. He told Papa and Papa told me, Tom's the smart one, Tom's the deep one.

I'm ignorant, Anna.

You keep that ignorance; that's all right, Tom; that's enough. How many babies you pulled? How many lives you saved? You keep that kind of ignorance. But I always thought, if there'd been money, there'd be more for your mind to chew on.

I wanted to be a doctor. But you always wanted to think worst of all. A doctor's a man of action. You're too deep.

Do you remember Eustacia Ardoin?

Of course I do. I used to walk to school with her older sister.

I think I always wanted to be like Eustacia. She let her dreams lead her. I always wanted…

Listen, wait a minute. You hear that?

Yes.

It's a horse. Who's on a horse this late?

Paul's boy on John's horse.

What's the matter with that horse? It's out that way.

The dogs came out of the field and struck the lane, running.

What's the matter with that horse? Let's go quick.

They started to walk and the cries grew; Schilling started to run. He turned a corner of the lane around high grass.

Go back. Go back. Get help quick. Anna turned and ran with the pace of one forty, slowed to a fast walk.

Woven in barbed wire like spoiled knitting the horse lay treading the air violently, a tall Negro kicking the horse's head, the head swimming like a fish, blood across the Negro's eyes, the horse varnished in blood, the throat of the horse pumping blood, the bright syrup on mahogany of horse and boy, the boy anguished, trying to kill the horse with his bare feet.

Get out of here, he told the boy. Run!

He threw off his coat, looked around for anything. There wasn't a rock, not a single device. The sound was terrible. He tried to pull up a fence post. The horse kicking in that agony nothing can record, he straddled the horse's neck, his leg thrown across the horse's face, hooking the nose with his knee, taking a quick purchase with the other leg. As though at a fish he began with a strand of the barbed wire to saw at the neck of the horse near the shoulders, his knee holding the flailing head. He used all of his strength until he saw the white juice in the blood and the horse tremble and quieten, snot pouring with blood on the grass. What good will that snot do you now, he thought. Then the horse was still. He stood up, his knees half bent, trembling, his trousers bloody, his hands bleeding. After a moment he dropped the strand of wire and stood up straight, crying. He unstraddled the horse and wept and wept and wept until he saw the dogs lying in the grass side by side in tongue-lolling companionship.

IV

O *Mary had appeared at the door when like a spider the sun had finished its web. Bearing greetings and a wash basin of warm water, she left the basin on a table beside soap and towels. First he shaved, then he washed his body, the long, depleted mummy of a man silent and white in the bright morning. The hair of his chest was gray, the shriveled penis, seat of so much fantastic glory, was hidden in a nest of gray. Gradually he had lost a hundred and fifty pounds. Some lingering flesh was jowelly across his chest, stretching and returning as though crawling.*

He had his shot and ate his breakfast. As the boarders left, some of them would pop their heads into the door for the morning greeting, leaving quickly. He felt quite good after breakfast, sat up in bed and looked around for some way to amuse himself. He decided he would get up and sit in the chair next to the window beside the aspidistra. He waited for Mary to come to clear the breakfast dishes.

How are you feeling? she asked.

I feel like getting up. Yessir, I'm going to get up and sit in that chair.

Now be careful. He swung his legs onto the footstool, inert levers or wheelless skates they seemed, twins of inertia clinging to each other almost effetely. But they worked, though he was a little woozy from the morphine and the change of position; he took four good steps to the chair, turned delicately, and eased himself into it.

Feels good.

She draped a blanket over his legs and said, What can I get you?

There's a book here. Nothing.

She put a small dinner bell beside his chair, and fresh water. Life was complete.

Now you ring.

Thank you, Mary.

Mary's kindness was boundless and profoundly gentle, though her speech was abrupt. He had learned to detect gentleness despite its masks, and since gentleness was his favorite art, the essence of his profession, he respected it as one expert respects another.

What he wanted was to look outside. Now that he was alone, like a child with candy, with enormous eagerness he turned his eyes toward the green of the world. It was fantastic. The color. The distance. The depth. He blinked for a moment recognizing common objects. It was as though it had been gone and returned, the lawn, the trees, the plants. After the green, he saw the sundry browns of autumn, and finally their shades. Details followed, several-colored leaves, stalks with darker shadows along them as though penciled in. Last, he saw insects, or traces of them. It was amazing. He thought of how in the development of the human fetus there was a hint of all evolution, as though pregnancy were a photograph of the history of life. Now, his perception returning was like a photograph of the development of perception, from the general to the specific. Amazing. But more simply he was content to accept the generalization of form and color.

For half an hour he looked out as though he were seeing the world for the first time. Thinking of how deviate intelligence is, craving for so much, and so quickly surfeit, requiring variety and change if only for an instant, he turned toward a book lying on the table beside him. At that moment he heard a sound on the lawn. Someone was rolling a lawnmower.

They came into view, Obadiah Johnson and Pluyey Martin, and stopped outside his window with the lawnmower and a file apiece. The first floor of the house was high, a good six feet, so that he was at least ten feet above them. Pluyey started to file the mower blade.

Niggah, you cain't fahl that thang lahk that.

Obie, hold th' blade still.

Pluyey, you're crazy. You know that?

Hold th' blade!

Wheah'd you evah git a name lahk Plooey? Booey. Hooey. Umph!

Wheah'd you evah git a name like Obba-dier. Humh?

You crazy, Pluyey.

Hold th' blade.

I cain't.

How come you cain't?

I'm fagged out just watchin' you.

Hold th' blade.

Now look heah. You get me offa comforble breadbox downair th' sto' to come up heah to do what? Mow th' lawn? What for? The winter's goin' kill th' grass.

Fo' money. Hold th' blade.

Money? What for? You don't need no money.

Miss Mary'll give us three dollars, three big 'mericans fo' her yawd.

Pluyey. Pluyey. Pluyey. What you want with three big American

— 39

dollars? Humh?

Hold th' blade.

Naw.

You don't want fifty cents of that?

Humph!

Seventy-five? Six bits.

Humph!

A dollah. Tha's all. No more.

Wham I'm goin' do with a dollah?

How I know what you goint do with a dollah?

What kin a man buy with a dollah?

How I know what you goin' t' buy?

Dollah anahalf?

What you goin' buy with foah bits more?

Mah business.

All right. Hol' de blade.

The blade is held. Pluyey.

Yeah?

Pluyey. Honey.

Don' honey me!

I just want ask you one thing, Pluyey. Pluyey?

Yes!

Pluyey, do you know sumpin'? I bet you didn't know this. I know you didn't know this. Pluyey honey, did you know that you can hold the blade by yoself?

Hold th' goddamned blade! Whatsa mattah with you? You crazy?

Almost got yo' finger cut off, didn't you?

Niggah, you are crazy!

Let go of it, didn't I. Cut you, Pluyey honey? There's a doctor living in theah. Maybe he kin help you. Can't hep hisself. Maybe he kin hep you. Now whoa! C'mon. Pluyey.

Put the file down. Please? Did I ever show you what's buried here? I buried it mahself. Please, Pluyey; put th' file down. I buried somethin'....

What?

You ain't mad?

Whut you buried?

You ain't goin' be mad no more?

Obie, goddammit, you're the damnedest man. What you buried?

What I get if I show you?

You get this file if you don't.

All right. C'mon.

Wheah?

Round here the back.

This shore better be somethin'.

C'mon, quit your fussin'.

You lead me round by the nose. I don't know why I got you for a frien'. Always sumpin'. He went off mumbling, following the younger Negro.

They vanished from the frame of the window. Schilling was curious about what Obadiah had buried, as he had been amused by the conference at which he was a foreigner. Negroes seldom speak freely around white people. He tried to recall when he had ever talked openly to a Negro in his lifetime, or since he was a child. In this manner his mind fell on Eustacia Ardoin as it had not except in casual moments of introspection since he had seen her on the streets of Dallas ten years before. He had decided her place long before and abandoned her again as the mind will in search of greater relevance. Too many faces had obscured her, and the pivot of experience in which a doctor stands, a point in human action and fortuity incomparably less sheltered than the life of anyone else, a point closer to blood and coarse fact than any other, had overwhelmed his personal right to reverie. He had seen many times that the practice of medicine and thought were the most compatible, each giving rise to the other. The combination evoked the tragic sense and a shame of ignorance incredible to bear. It gave rise to an ethic never practical, an imperative duty that the sauntering delusive dreamers in their generalization of organism would never obey. Sedated against knowledge by every madness of the mind, they, not even in their moments of death, could contemplate the horrible complexity of any life or any matter, and lived among processes that were limited by themselves, and inevitably doomed with an authority horrible to conceive. And he among them except for certain moments of clarity when he accepted death and its complexity with a partial notion of how enormous the scale is and how it expands, this sojourn of atoms and particles and its lonely collections. He thought of the humane as the recognition of mortality against the scale of whatever was knowable, neither more nor less. His mind had been confined by its ignorance, and from it his frustration had risen: the ignorance of today, not of ten years hence. With the knowledge of ten years hence he could have worked miracles. To that extent it was relative. The practice of medicine and thought is hounded with a succession of if's bearable only by illusion or madness.

Too much experience, no matter how much he thought, too much too close. He did not now think of Eustacia Ardoin with the abruptness memory forces with its dead relevance into idleness. He thought only of a Negro woman named Rosalie, then thought of something else, crossing his legs casually, at once thinking of it as a strange gesture. He had placed the ankle of his right leg over his left knee with the flair of a hearty man thirty years younger. Strange. He was indeed feeling well. Very good. He would enjoy it. He picked up the book and began to read, glancing out of the window again at the world.

TO WALK ALONE down night lanes in the thirties; to see boles, cattle, primroses white in the starlight; to hear insects calling from village to village; to smell the sky, hunt the bears, look for the Southern Cross, to watch the white tide of our galaxy rise in the early evening, a river of worlds; to stop barefoot in the sand and listen for a dog far away, a jersey's cudding, her grunt and belch and poof, the sound of a car, its lights following in reflection, highlands far in the distance, the sound of a windmill catching the breeze, the sound of night alone.

THE SOUND OF LEATHER, footfall of pferd, creaking wheel, the knight drowned in the river, his cheek on the blue horse's haunch. Away. The shore-fires are dead, the companions asleep. Tomorrow, next week, in a year, the open sea. Footfall of pferd, a wheel creaking, a buggy coming. He switched his satchel from hand to hand and waited. The knight spun toward the sea, out of sight. Away. He heard a dog bark. There was no light but for the stars. No moon. The three houses, east, northeast and west had stanched their wicks. A well pulley creaked. Someone had come for a last drink of water out of the dark well, water falling to its mother-eye from a leaking bucket. He slowed for the buggy's approach. His hand was raw from the grip handle, but he wanted to reach beyond the house where the farmer stood at the porch drinking and surveying the fields and road, a figure inferred but who nevertheless stood among the dark trees. Finally he heard the horse snort. Past the farmhouse he stopped, his shoes the color of sand, the color of the road. He put down the grip and took his watch from his vest; he had been walking for an hour. He brushed his wet forehead and removed his glasses by their right rim, turning his head as they came off. He took a rose colored handkerchief from his vest and wiped them. He removed his hat and wiped his balding head, hurrying now, the horse near.

His heart was slowing; he hadn't noticed it was beating fast.

He got the glasses on and waved his hat and called, Monsieur! Monsieur!

Eh? Who's there?

Dr. Schilling. Who is it?

Radin Fontenot. Ho up! Whoah! Whoa horse!

Did you pass my horse?

No, Doctor. I have come from Cousin Paul's.

Then you haven't come that far. He has a bad foot. I left him a mile this side of Faubian's place.

Quiet! Ho! Get in. Give me your bag. Your hand, Doctor. Whoa … whoa ….

I'm glad you came along. My feet are very sore.

I'll take you into town. Faubian's wife?

Yes.

Hi! *Jk jk*! Boy or girl? Take the sand out of your shoe.

Mrs. Faubian died.

Oh? Shake it good. What was the trouble?

What was the trouble? Too young? Too old? Too fat? Too lean? Too weak? Unclean? Too soon? Too late? A thirty-year-old Frenchwoman mother of three with one loss from miscarriage. Dead. Bleeding? Ordinary. Ready? Spontaneous birth, head forward. A perfect birth, the child normal. After cleaning her, checking her pulse dozens of times, after washing his hands while rolling his sleeves down he sat on the bed speaking to her, telling her it was all right, a girl, and she would be brought in a moment. Perhaps three minutes, sorting his bag, perhaps five He sat down on the bed again and she was dead. Death seen not in stillness merely but in a freezing of stature, a lapse of personality, a fixation in time as thorough as wind-blown grass. He thought in that instant he had not finished his conversation with Anna the year before: gone. Her mouth was open slightly, one eye glinting past the aperture of the lid. He reached for the heart; it wasn't there. Her wrist; it was gone. Her throat; it was gone. He tried; he tried. He called somebody while trying, but it was gone. He quizzed them sharply and found that she had been canning early peaches before her pains started, and for every three, she would eat one. She'd died of indigestion, without making a distinction between the pains of birth and the pains of peaches. She had told him nothing; he hadn't asked. She died of canning peaches, he said to Fontenot.

Eh?

She worked too hard; didn't take care of herself.

The horse juggled on, his feet like balls in the air. There was a breeze in the movement; it was a hot night, by date still spring. They drove into a grove of pine trees, and beyond, fields of rice, fields of corn. The rice fields, flat and dark, even the corn catching the light of the stars. The Milky Way, like a banner, or river, or sea, as bright as a moon. Now to a forest where the horse snorted and picked up his trot. Beyond were dim lights from the town.

I'm sorry to take you beyond your place, Mr. Fontenot.

I will enjoy the excuse to drink a little wine at Percell's. Do you drink a little wine, Doctor?

Yes.

My wife doesn't care for me to drink it unless it's a special occasion. I've heard that your wife opposes all drinking.

That's not true, entirely.

Like my wife she has religious principles. I suppose they don't want to see anyone go to excess, which is a good thing, no? I suppose those who go to excess would know when they had. I think I'll have a glass of wine with you, Mr. Fontenot.

I was going to ask you.

Two more farm houses east and south, then the road bent north through more woods until the houses arose on the outskirts of the town, lights still burning after ten o'clock. A blacksmith and stable, an abandoned grocery, a bar for Negroes, then dark businesses facing each other across hardpacked streets; past his office, the bank, the dentist's, a mercantile, a drugstore, a dress shop, through the town to Percell's. Except for one buggy waiting outside, the streets were empty.

Even in those days he didn't want to go home. His wife was asleep and though he wasn't prone to talk, he needed the presence of a consciousness which ferreted his pain. The death of the woman stayed with him, the pasteurization of her face as clear as an image carved in onyx. Yet he thought of Anna and that he hadn't seen her in the year since they had walked in the fields at Abbeville. He thought of Anna, some presage of a later date, an engagement in onyx. The thought hurried out of his mind to the pure reality of the nail-gray face of the woman growing in death. How quickly death grows! Sperm and ova crawl toward each other casually and their formality becomes engrossed with itself over a period of months. Yet in half an hour the face is nailed irrecoverably. Life is inflated tissue immediately abandoned by its damned forces. He didn't want to be alone. He walked with Fontenot into the same tavern where Ardoin had lain dead over the table; thinking of Anna.

Gilles! Two wines. The doctor's horse broke his foot. Mrs. Faubian is dead of childbirth.

Faubian! Dr. Schilling. What was the matter? Red? He poured the wine quickly and came to their table, turned a chair and sat down, leaning forward against its back. What was the matter, Dr. Schilling?

Overwork.

Overwork? Fontenot, overwork?

The doctor says….

She didn't know when to quit.

Oh my goodness. I'm sorry to hear. Dr. Schilling, how did your horse break his leg?

He overworked too.

How far did you have to walk?

He walked from a mile this side of Faubian's to two miles from town.

Five miles. I am sorry for Faubian. I didn't know the Mrs., but Faubian is a good man. How is he?

He's taking it tough, Schilling said.

I'm sorry. It'll be at the Protestant church, your church, Doctor? Yes.

I'm sorry. This is only the second time you've been in my place, Doctor. You seem to come with death. When Eustacia killed her husband?

I remember.

She was crazy. Of course she was crazy. You were right. That woman should not have suffered more than her insanity.

The bar was lit with candles against the liquor bottles and lamps on several tables. A deer's head hung from a pillar, the saliva of the deer stilled, yet to drip on the stove beneath its muzzle, unlit since February. The room had rugs from the backs of river deer. When Ardoin had died, the floor had been of sawdust.

But it's very hard to tell if a person's crazy. I think a lot of people are crazy; a lot of people think I'm crazy.

Only your wine is crazy, Percell, Fontenot said.

Maybe it makes you crazy, Fontenot. I must say, Fontenot, you are a sane drinker. He's sensible, Doctor. He feels good, he talks, then he goes home. But we don't know you so well, Dr. Schilling....

I pass your place very often going on calls at night....

You work while we play. I suppose a doctor's work is never done. Fontenot might work hard, but I think when he leaves here he goes by to see Rosalie. After all, she's half white.

Agh!

I don't know. To hell with our joking; will you forgive it, Doctor?

Does anyone know her last name? Schilling asked.

Good God, who knows, the bartender said.

Simpson, Fontenot said.

Are you sure?

No, Fontenot said.

How many children is she supporting?

Four, Fontenot said.

Are you sure?

No, Fontenot said.

She's too young, too preserved to have four children. Dr. Schilling, have you ever treated her?

How could he answer? For what?

For anything.

No, not for just anything.

Dr. Schilling is a very quiet man, known for his silence. I understand she comes to your office often....

Sometimes.

And somebody had beat her? The bartender was open-eyed.

That or there was an earthquake.

I see. This has happened before? Eh? Dr. Schilling, you are a very reluctant man. Nevertheless, Rosalie is a part of all of us, isn't she?

Fontenot groaned and drank all of his wine. If she were whiter, Fontenot said, and licked his empty glass.

I saw her with a bruise across her face, the bartender said. Schilling was silent.

Dr. Schilling isn't going to talk, the bartender said, leaving his chair to refill the glasses of three men sitting beyond the stove. Fontenot rose and went to the bar placing his glass on the mahogany, leaning forward, saying, I think you ought to be less familiar with the doctor.

Why? the bartender said.

I like to sit with him and you should respect him more.

I don't disrespect him. I'm only making conversation.

I think it would be better not to force him to leave. He doesn't come here often, does he?

Ahh! Dr. Schilling, I'm going to buy us all three glasses of wine. Schilling was sitting with his back to them, having heard their conversation. He was, had been, a tall enough man, slender in his youth, but now he was bent over yielding to weight that wasn't yet paunch but that was tired, his crown showing a small egg of balding covered over with the combing of his hair, still black and always straight. From the back he would have struck no one as having either dignity or being an exception. The eggy crown with its nakedness, pink and partially webbed over with stray hairs; the back, rounded lazily, tiredly, his shoulders suggesting the retreat of a turtle; one leg outside the shadow of the table, a fourth of its calf showing along with sock-garters; all contributed to anonymity, or the portraiture of a casual painter who sketches drinkers. That painter would have sketched him, however, because of the size of the head and the smoothness of the neck and the way he fingered the empty glass. He was a big man, the leg was too large to be exposed, and his entire figure too meditative for simple tiredness. A painter might have recognized that there was an absence of conscious posture and, with the incongruity of his size and his structure amid the clothes of his class, become curious at the thought this tension of the neck and the floating fingering of the glass betrayed. Yet there was nothing extraordinary about him to those around him but his status and some sense of his reputation.

Schilling smiled when the bottle of wine was placed on the table with three fresh glasses, admitting the two men by leaning back and shifting his leg under the table, his trouser leg covering the garter. He left them to talk, prepared to endure whatever tone of casualness thoughtless men are capable of. He found anything less than confrontation a damned lie, and he found a lack of seriousness an anemia of intelligence, or an opiate. In the presence of recognition there are convictions of mind; in the absence of recognition there is neither mind nor conviction but some clever substitute, a spasmic laughter, a turning away or a cursory denial by fragmentation of images; laughter is a fragmentation of the whole, its response a response to incompleteness, and by its nature a denial of intelligence. Cousin to trivia, both a lack of courage, a final mask, the ultimate mask worn against the fires: time, process, impotence.

Dr. Schilling, it is so good to have you here. I will never forget the night you came here and found Ardoin dead. I saw him die, I think. He was very nervous—after he had eaten the cakes—jittery, jumping around, having a fit. Then with a jolt he hit his head on the table, vibrating—you know—and thump! He was dead. Not a move. Motionless. It all happened so quickly; first he vomited, the dry heaves, then the fits. He was smiling!

Yes, Schilling said. He had wondered many times why Ardoin hadn't tasted the strychnine on the cakes, but the cakes contained black walnuts that were stale. Eustacia's brothers had brought the walnuts from northern Louisiana the fall before; that had been established in court. Why kill him? He denied the emotions, but he accepted the equation. Closed! The matter is closed these three years. At least he didn't want to talk about it now. Yet he was interested in the way any other mind saw anything.

Did you think he had been poisoned by the time it took him to die? Schilling asked.

No! I thought he had had apoplexy.

Apoplexy! Indeed. Eighteenth century, perhaps a little later, Schilling thought.

When did you decide he was poisoned?

Why, when you said it.

And you thought only of apoplexy?

Of course.

Then why did you say afterward, before I had fully examined him, that he had been poisoned?

Did I say that?

Yes.

When?

Before the deputy came, you said it to me.

Well …. The mystery I suppose. Everyone knows his wife is

crazy. But I'll be honest with you, Doctor: everyone knew Ardoin was a roamer. Everyone knew where he had roamed ....

Rosalie? Schilling asked.

For a long moment the bartender eyed Schilling with calculation, and deciding he had to live in the same town with his mortality upon the scalepan of the only doctor, the bartender shattered his concepts by laughing. Rosalie, of course. Who else? That whore....

Schilling was grateful to cowardice once again. The Paddie, gone these three years, had not told him what the town had known.

Do you think that's a reason to kill a man?

Reason? What reason? What does reason have to do with killing a man?

Suddenly Schilling replied, I like you Percell.

And suddenly Percell locked his eyes with Schilling's, either no longer alone. For only an instant, a part of the look a study of what this moment could lead to; nothing; there was no sense of application in the mind of Percell, and Schilling had seen the same lapse of look before.

Nevertheless, I like you, Percell. I must go.

You haven't drunk your wine, Dr. Schilling, Percell said, regretful and dubious about himself.

Nevertheless....

Percell wanted to do something about it but he had lost his opportunity. He felt lost, watching the tall man rising from his suited flowing into the chair, ignoring the half glass of wine. Fontenot sat there as though studiously choosing condiments. As though putting a coat on, that pause, that kind of pause, Schilling waited, then abruptly picked his bag from the floor and left. Percell sighed and jostled Fontenot who raised the bottle and poured a drink.

With his grip he stepped out of the light and in twenty paces was alone under the stars, Percell's bar remote, a thing to behold from a point of virgin thought, as though never seen before.

ALONE ON EVENINGS, caught out in the night, the hunter with inadequate eyes plodding through a sandy lane without that immorality of self-consciousness, without even knowledge or reference for his thoughts. Willows growing by no river, windmills turning in no wind. What is it? An incapacity to swim through all seen, or to fly, or to swallow the willows, the fields, the sky, the stars, the night in its millions of suggestions that one is alive. Eyeless as Samson, a mind seven years out of its womb, already grasping that life is too much to bear, too strange and enormous. To walk night lanes at the age of seven, the frogs clicking around the edge of tanks, or a bullfrog croaking in the grass making you jump. To be alone after dark coming home from playing, barefoot and free under the May stars. To step in cold cow dung and wipe it off in the grass like a cripple dragging his foot. He wanted to stay out under the stars forever, yet he was afraid and he wanted to get home; he didn't know what he wanted. He saw the windmill now and heard its chains as some breeze turned not the wheel, but the rudder against its setting. Beyond the lane past the cow pen lay the house in the trees, dark among the cypresses. He stopped to look at the stars, letting his head fall back till he almost fell. That was fun, dizzying fun. He stumbled a little, got his bearings and raised his face to the highest stars; and he fell. And lay there looking up at the stars. He sniffed. Couldn't smell them. Something else got in the way of whatever scent the stars might have. He reached with his hand in back of his head groping like a crab in the grass. Cow shit. He wiped it off on the grass, the rest on his overalls. He reached with his hand all around him. None. Then he scooted with his heels and butt a foot down the lane; two feet, feeling for cow dung with his toes. Now with the dignity of Palomar moving at twilight, he panned the skies swallowing the galaxy gradually. It was not enough. He opened his eyes wider, naming the constellations he knew: the bears, Orion, Bootes. That wasn't what he wanted to do. He wanted to gobble the world, the stars, the wind. It was painful, fleeting, but always returning. A cow lowed. Ernest had long ago milked. The windmill creaked; a May wind had risen, and lay down again. He looked beyond the fence where the house lay. He could see the porch light reflecting in the trees. He thought he heard his name. He looked again at the stars, raising his ankle to his knee to scratch. Mosquitoes. He rested his leg on his knee looking for the figures in the sky which seemed to have moved. He heard somebody coming. No; it was a cow grazing beyond the fence. Again he looked for the figures; had they moved? It didn't seem likely; stars don't move. Not that fast. He had lost them, let them become mixed with other groups to where they had no shape. He must imagine very hard. There, there was a bear. Now the others fell into place. Why only bears and hunters? Silly question. They could be anything if you took the time to make them anything. He could see a dragon down the middle of the Milky Way; he could see a tarantula crawling out of the sky in the south. That he didn't like. He started to feel around in the grass to make sure there were none about to crawl on him. He didn't like feeling around in the grass either. Again he heard something; this time someone was coming. Someone barefoot, their heels hitting in the hard sand with a thumping. He rolled over to lie in the grass at the edge of the road. Here they come looming. It was Jessie Lee taking the milk home to his mother, the Negro woman who had cared for him since he was born and from whose house he should have returned before dark rather than be lying on the bending Johnson grass watching the figure coming dumbly thumping. He knew it was Jessie Lee and had thought of jumping out into the road to scare the boy twice his age and had thought that wouldn't be a good thing to do for two reasons: first, it hurt to be scared; second, Jessie Lee was twice his size and milk pails are heavy this time of night. Yet knowing it was Jessie Lee, even about to call his name, some science of the long night of men crawling into now was left in his quick and he was terrified. For an instant, as though chased and about to die and already dying by thousands of terrors, his heart hit his chest crudely, then stopped, and began beating again deliberately as though a pounder at a door demanding to be let out. Jessie Lee was past before young Schilling could hear anything again but his heart inside his ears. It was suddenly cool, sweat on his forehead, and he thought of hurrying home; but he rolled over to look at the stars again listening for his heart, remembering that was always the last thing he heard at night before he went to sleep. Old Orion.

THE LIGHT FROM PERCELL'S now behind the corner of a building, he looked up at the stars. Orion was clear tonight, exceptionally bright. His grandfather had taught him the constellations, first the bears, the pole star, the Pleiades, Cygnus, Cassiopeia, Orion. His father had not taught him; his father had little to do with knowledge or the less than obvious, but his grandfather, that scholar with his poetry and Greek-populated mind, had vibrated like timbals on his ear with legends and names as though he, the old man, had lived them himself and had spoken the names into vanished ears. Schilling stopped for a moment in the totally dark town reminded of his grandfather and of how after the old man's death he, Schilling, would lie in a cornfield and think of the old man by counting and naming the constellations thus telling over to himself the moment he had first heard them.

One night looking up through tall June corn at Orion three years or more after his grandfather's death, the thought suddenly occurred that that old man so rotted in the damp Louisiana earth had actually seen these same stars, collecting them into the figure of a hunter. Why, Grandpapa, don't we ever see the gods and titans anymore? They have retired, the old man had said. Lying in the field where he had gone to move his bowels before going to bed he saw the moon toward the west, and the thought took him with a shock that that moon was the only thing he could imagine every person who had ever lived had seen. He shivered for a moment before he pursued the thought: that every person who had ever lived (and before, while still arboreal) had seen that moon, and it was all he and they had laid eyes on in common. Numbing. Marvelous. Numbing.

He moved down the dark street toward his office where he hadn't opened his mail. He sat in the noisy leather swivel chair and slit the envelopes from drug companies, dropping them into the wastebasket. There was a letter from Anna of two paragraphs in which she said she was coming home from Missouri and would like to spend some time with them. He was delighted, he had heard from her only twice since she had gone to St. Louis to attend a business school, Anna quite certain there was room for an unmarried woman in a firm in New Orleans or Dallas or Houston. He answered the letter immediately and placed the envelope in a wireworm for pencils to be mailed in the morning. He looked around the office with its dark cedar cabinets and still photographs, through the door to the black leather examining table not quite beyond the light of the lamp on his desk. His books took one wall to the left of where he sat, the sets of books MacFarland had said for him to buy, the set MacFarland had given him. The Scot walking with him with that lack of poise of European man down the streets of Louisville in dirty dark trousers with old blood among their stains, talking not only of anatomy but of forms themselves of which anatomy was a small study, but a deforming study, dissolving the forms that sum to make the form of man. However far ye take doon, to a vessel, a cell, or even an atom, it isn't relevant unless it's man. Not because man is so relevant, but he's the greatest collection of all of these, and he's the one asking the questions anyhow. And about how European man had spread over the world and when would he retreat as retreat he must. To MacFarland America from Tierra del Fuego to the Bering Sea was Europe, except for its grasses and a few animals. It was the beginning of a long night, nights of sitting in his office remembering MacFarland, the books to the left of him whenever possible, thinking of MacFarland as an anchor that slowly gave way over the years; the nights merging and forming the anatomy of night before and after both wars until that moment when his first heart attack occurred, even when he lived without the books moving from brother to brother, the books stored in some distant town, thinking at night all of his life of MacFarland, first of MacFarland, then of the books and MacFarland, then of the books MacFarland had signed, then of the books and how he used to think of the books and think of MacFarland, then of how at night instead of going home he would remain where the books were, not thinking of them, and so on, until the sense of the books, the books, and MacFarland, were remote but connected, the anchor dragging in the drift of time. He blew out the light, spun the swivel chair in leaving and locked the door.

Not walking home he turned left and passed Percell's still lit and walked to where the road turned north. Beyond Percell's the town was totally dark and in a few minutes he was beyond the sense of hulk, the starlight reflecting on roofs and buildings. A sandy road again, the northern leg of the road he had walked from Faubian's. He had forgotten his bag, or left it as a gesture to a wish not to be called again. Anna was coming before long, by mid-summer. He loved her; she was the only woman he had ever loved sensibly, without homage or obeisance or any constant sense of debt. The agony with Quero is hard to word, such an intelligent creature but always only suggested as vocal chords suggest voice. Her form, a shrine of lust, yet empty of joy and bells of lust, or peals of laughter; enjoyed but joyless; brilliant, but lacking crystal; fertile, but with no odor; open but enveloped. She had not *become*, or she had become on some track he knew nothing of. Anna he loved comfortably without any sense of having to sustain anything: there: always there. His grandfather had talked of women and love, and of woman, Circe, Melpomene, Venus, Helen, Alceste, Psyche, that old man licking the world on his chops and all its men had imagined. And MacFarland had once delicately shown Schilling the cadaver of a young woman whose face he had never forgotten, its hair long and still, pasted from the perspiration of dying against her cheek, loose and about to fall from any movement, perfect and portrait. Her body slender and warmly portrayed, the death from some illness as shameful as a burst spleen. Reverently, not only for knowledge, MacFarland had gently pried open her vulva catching the discharge on a piece of cotton and said, Ye see how perfectly she's made. D'ye see, Young Doctor, she's made perfectly. See how complete she is. What moor in the name of man or nature could ye ask for. There is perfection named by purpose. And Schilling could add, there are losses of senses of form.

Orion brilliant, unbelievably brilliant, the rest of the galaxy clear, clean dust with edges. He thought once of stars through the mind of Eustacia whom he realized he loved as quietly as Anna, of her view of the stars through the bars of her mad cell; he thought of valid love asking no price, beautifully asking no price, marvelously asking no price.

Dead leaves from the autumn past, engrossed with sand, clotted the ditches beyond the town, storm on autumn, storm on autumn on autumn, turns of the year burying each other. The cattle lowing. He reached the cemetery where the obelisks stand like icicles in the night. He cupped his hands on a cedar post, his foot resting on a strand of barbed wire, and saw the flat stone of his firstborn between two pylons of granite. He had thought of everything that still lived in him, yet he dreamed most of a child to whom he could someday talk. On the night after she had died he had taken this walk beyond town and stood with one foot on the barbed wire, his hands cupped on the post like a rider with stirrup and pommel, the flat shadow between the masts of forgotten men, the stone unlaid. He had stood for an hour that spring, and suddenly he looked up, and there flew a sperm across the sky: the comet of 1910.

HE SAW A BRIGHTNESS in the southeast that made him think a shooting star had fallen, and turned his face, his cheek against the grass, and saw a mile away fire in a field or beyond. Again terror, true terror, he rose and ran. The horizon was boiling red, sparks against the stars, rising, competing with them. He shot like a streak up the lane as only a child can run, not getting anywhere too fast but all of him moving faster than anything alive except a hummingbird. Sport was barking at the fire as he flew past, barking in alarm and panic. In the house his father was standing bleeding, his glasses broken. His mother held a crutch over her shoulder like a bat while leaning on the other one. His father was trying to wipe the blood from his eyes. She threatened him with the crutch. He was trying to ease the broken lens from its frame with his fingers. Webber wasn't there. He had blood over his tie and coat, the blood gushing from his forehead into his eye. She swung the crutch with force and missed him. He stepped back, bending his head, blinded. She swung the crutch again and though he couldn't see it coming, he stepped back for balance, the crutch missing him accidentally. All of this in the time it took the child to pass through the kitchen and cross the room running.

Fire!

Where? she said.

What fayah? he said.

Toward Mr. Wolf's.

Oh my God, she said.

He moved quickly through the kitchen out the back door. The boy followed. She grabbed the crutches properly and rode them. He and the boy ran across the yard beyond the barn. The yard lights went on.

Quero, please turn out those lights.

I need them to see.

All right. Son, go turn them out as soon as your mother gets here.

What is it? What is it? she said, swinging on those crutches.

It looks like one of Wolf's barns.

Can't you tell? Why don't you help me like a white man would?

He moved to help her and she thrust him aside.

My God, my God, it's one of his barns. Her gray eyes were lean in the light of the fire.

Turn out the light, son, he said.

Where's my big boy? she said. Where's he? Where is he?

Tom, go find Webber. He's in his room studying.

They were left alone, watching the fire. The doctor re-folded the handkerchief to a dry place and mopped his forehead gingerly.

I've got to do something about this.

About what? she asked,

I've got to go in. This cut is still bleeding.

You're not going in and leave me alone...?

Well, Quero, it's bleeding.

Let it bleed. You ought to bleed a little. I wonder what caused it?

Has he been storing silage?

What's that?

Green hay will cause a fayah; or wet hay.

Well I declare.

Young Schilling came with his brother, a lean dark boy at the apex of his teens, the bright dark Webber troubled in his visage. as always, around the two of them.

I've got to go in, the doctor said, turning toward the house.

Dad, what's the matter? Webber asked. His brown eyes warm and pained, identical to his father's, the brows the same, furrowed and black.

Take care of your mother; don't let her fall. He left.

I saw it first out in the lane.

Where were you? Webber asked.

Where were you? His mother asked.

Playing with Curly.

Where is Curly?

Home.

You were at Curly's house?

Yes Mother.

I thought you were in the house. I thought I heard you in the living room listening to the radio. I don't want you at Curly's house after dark, do you hear?

I was playing the radio, Mother, Webber said.

I thought you were in your room studying.

Look at the sparks!

Poor Mr. Wolf. Do you think they'll set anything else afire?

I don't think so, Webber said.

But Webber, you don't know!

I don't think so, Mother; I don't think so. He said it with that mortal beautiful quiet, a serenity that infected everyone, even his mother, quieting her most of the time. It was something no one could escape, and many thought that was all there was to Webber. Young Schilling felt secure now that Webber was here.

(What's the matter with Dad?)

Are you talking to me? Why're you whispering? Who're you talking to? Well, Webber, you know how he treats me. Do you know he tried to go to his office tonight because he said he couldn't stand it here anymore with me? Imagine. I stood in the door and he tried to move me. Hmph! Let him bleed. He ought to be shot and cut! Her fierce gray eyes mocked back at the fire with their own madness.

Look at the sparks.

He's bleeding? Webber said.

Where are you going?

Inside.

Leave me standing here? All right! All right! I've got my boy here who'll take care of me. Won't you, Tommy?

Aren't the stars beautiful, Mother?

I ought to go in and call Mr. Wolf. Help me in. Careful.

He tore away from the fire and walked beside her, not able to help her but keeping the dog off.

The doctor had brought his grip from the car, stood stanching the bleeding over the kitchen sink. She and the boy passed him and Webber standing there without a word, Webber offering a clean damp cloth, young Schilling glancing at his father with shame, drifting beyond them with his mother swinging on the crutches like one of the horsemen—plague, war, famine, or death—wanting to stay and do something or just watch both of them in complete tune.

A moment later, each in their rooms, still perspiring and the pain from the cut sharp, he walked out to where they had stood. The fire had subsided, the recollection of its brightness irrelevant. The light went out in his wife's room. He was tired. The dog put its cold nose in his hand, its body against his knee as warm as blood. He turned to walk toward the house, patting the dog, looking up at the stars, amazingly brilliant. He heard the windmill; a wind had risen. The galaxy was spread against the sky, its nonsense burning brightly.

HE AWAKENED in the midst of a dream that night and was unable to sleep until just before he heard the cook waving the bell for breakfast.

Docta' Schilling, theer's a man at the do'.

Who is it?

He don't say. He says you got to come.

I'll be right there. Picking the socks beside the bed, still with sand in them, not waiting for others, wherever they would come from in a hurry, his wife long ago risen, he sought frantically to hurry, to be efficient, leaning into emergency. Like a fool he sought to move expertly and in the middle of a reach sat down on the bed and looked at himself and asked, what has nature contrived now? What am I doing? What drama is this in which I'm caught? What is the conflict, what is the war, what are the issues, who started them, what am I doing? With unutterable depression he leaned down to tie his shoes. What is this battle? I'm going out there to hear, at the worst, death. A masque, or a charade. He tied his shoes and went forth. Morning.

Tell him I'll be right there.

The cook, her young maid absent, handed him a demitasse of coffee on the porch and a cup of poached egg which he swallowed. A Negro man was standing with one foot on the step, his hand on a porch pillar.

Dr. Schilling, suh, Rosalie sent me.

What's the matter with Rosalie?

She been cut.

Where is she?

Home.

The doctor got his bag while the Negro waited outside. They walked to the edge of town where the doctor had entered the night before with Fontenot. Rosalie lived in a shotgun shack, a building with one beam, one gable straddling it, built of harsh wood the color of gunpowder. Inside it had an odor of snuff and toilet water.

It had been divided into two rooms by cheap cloth hung from hooks. In the first was the cookstove and places to sit; in the second Rosalie lay on a bed amid crude furniture, under a purple quilt.

What's happened to you, girl?

I ain't no girl, Dr. Schilling. I been cut.

Young woman then.

I'm older than you are.

All right. Let's see. Where is it?

Get that nigger out of here. You go home now, LeBlanc. I'll call you.

He lifted the quilt, she helping him, an automatic instant of mutual pity making both their motions tender. She was in a flannel nightgown; she helped him pull the nightgown up. Underneath was a bloody piece of muslin folded approximately over her appendix, stuck to its clot. Gently he lifted it, careful, looking under the edge as he went. She winced and cussed in both English and French. She had a gash in her peritoneal cavity, well clotted but inflamed and not entirely closed. He took a probe from a test tube of alcohol and probed, careful of the clot.

Have you passed blood? She pointed to the slopjar beside the bed. Under the lid was a bloody black stool.

Who did this?

Never mind.

He opened the curtain made of cotton sacking. He set water to boil, and sat down to press her belly.

Hurt?

Shit! He gave her a sedative. He cleaned the wound while she gritted and cussed. She was a light Negress, her skin in places an incomparable yellow, though her face was rouged and powdered beyond color. Rosalie had been to his office several times for female examinations; she was always clean. Twice she had been there with severe bruises, but she would never admit to his guess that they were part of her trade. She was a defiant woman and there were legends about her, not only as the most desirable whore in town, but stories of where her white blood had come from; there was always an intimation that it was from high places. Rosalie was what southerners would call a 'smart nigger.' There were reasons for not starting a feud with her, and each man knew in his own heart what those reasons were.

She had been born on the Bayou Teche and had grown up in the north, the doctor thought around Cairo, Illinois. He was curious about her but he never made inquiries of her or anyone else. What he'd learned came from assumptions dropped by men on sidewalks in front of stores. He had the impression she was a strong woman and she had been cheated and knew it, and had come back to Mamou when she was grown as though to wait for justice. Beyond these things, he knew nothing more of Rosalie except that she seemed to look deeply into the doctor every time she saw him, as though both of them knew something about the world that could never be explained to anyone else.

When he finished cleaning the surface, she was quieter, breathing easier. He poured some tincture of opium into a small bottle and wrote directions on it.

Read these directions and take it when the pain gets bad. If the pain changes, call me immediately. If there's any change. Don't move, don't get out of bed except to use that, and if you can, wait. Do you hear? You may die. I'm going to send Livia from my house to sit with you.

Livia?

You know Livia. Ophelia's daughter.

Livia, huh?

She'll do what you say. Livia's young, but she's a good girl.

First she looked at him sternly, then her eyes changed to curiosity. She mis-shaped her mouth in study. After a time she said, You don't know, do you?

Know what?

Never mind.

I know you're suffering. You help me do all I can.

She looked away in contempt, pouting. He wrapped his instruments in a piece of gauze and put them in a paper sack.

Don't eat anything at all and don't drink any water. Until I tell you to. Do you hear? You may die if you don't listen to me.

He was moving toward the door. I'll come back at noon. You do what I've told you.

She turned her head toward him and studied him again. Thank you Dr. Schilling. You know Miss Eustacia couldn't kill anybody, don't you? You know that all the time, don't you?

Not in her right mind.

Not in no mind. But you don't know nothin', do you?

What do you mean?

Never mind. Just never mind.

You call me if there's any change. I'll come back at noon.

Thank you, Dr. Schilling. Thank you.

His wife was on the porch when he reached home, bending, cutting flowers growing in boxes hanging from the roof. He had bought the house and she had transformed the yard from a vegetable to a flower garden, the vegetables now growing in the back in a dozen long rows she had had plowed. The place looked like a home now; even the decorum of the boarders had changed, not toward respectability, but in the way of people who look forward to a little light in a dull world. The meals were no more formal, but there was more grace to them. The china was now tasteful, there was always a lace cloth at evening meals and on Sundays the food was served in polished silver.

Quero, I'm going to send Livia to take care of a patient for a day or two.

I was going to use her in the garden. Who's she taking care of?

A sick Negro woman. She's got to have somebody with her.

Of course it's all right. Is she very sick?

She may be very sick before it's all over,

Maybe I can go and help her.

Maybe you can. But for now, Livia will do.

He could seldom include Quero in his cases, not because of her sensitivity, but because she was too nervous. It wasn't a failure of character; it was the power of her nature to be given to exhilaration or despair. She rose to any necessity willingly, but she was never sustained in her rising by a quality which might keep her from feeling suffering too strongly. She had the empathy of an artist with none of the control of a professional who had to endure. It was not her past; it was her nature. When he put her with a patient because there was no one else, he regretted it afterward; her nervousness and depression were apparent for weeks. She never complained and she was always willing and he admired her courage.

Nothing was further from his cast of mind than the ways of a sleuth. He detested guessing among shifty assumptions, but he was highly capable of theory. He went to see the deputy that morning to ask him simply what constituted enough evidence for the re-opening of a case. Strong proof, witnesses, direct proof linking someone to a crime. That's what he had thought.

At noon he went to Rosalie's shack and found her with three degrees of temperature. He gave a thermometer to Livia, a girl of twenty or so, and left. Livia was inscrutable to him.

When he returned late in the afternoon, Rosalie had a temperature of 104. He gave her an alcohol bath, examined the wound, and went home to supper.

That night he sent Livia home for a few hours and sat with Rosalie. Livia became a half-wit the moment he spoke to her, with big rolling eyes. There was no way of telling whether it was real or not, so deeply she hid behind all masks. But from time to time when he had noticed her around his house—she had been there ever since Ophelia had come, long before the death of Ardoin; it was she who made the beds in the mid-mornings after her mother had left the house for two hours or so each day—he had thought there was an alert mind behind her masks. He was lost for a motive.

She became delirious around nine o'clock. At first he could make nothing out of her delirium. She was mixed up with her childhood along the Bayou Teche; then she was using the names of towns of Illinois. He felt silly listening to the babblings of a Negro whore as though.... She became less rambling for a time and he learned that her father was Eustacia's father. That revelation threw him completely off his quest. It sounded for a time that it was Rosalie who had resented the running of Ardoin. Then she began muttering, the doctor's house, the doctor's house, the doctor's house. He sat fingering the quilt, muslin-thin with clotted cotton, a terrible thing for a human being to lie under. Then through pity he saw envy, what enormous envy these people must have for all the whites of the world. Suddenly he went to his bag, pulled out a tray where there lay a dozen ampoules in a felt covering. He pulled out a vial of strychnine which he had not used for several years. It had been full when he had last seen it. Now there were three pills that showed above the felt, the three pills held in place with a kitchen match, the other thirty pills gone.

The next morning he told the deputy. The deputy said it couldn't be proved. Two days later Rosalie died of peritonitis. He had already sent Livia away.

The book kept him at peace until high morning, when the pain began to climb again. He thought each time it had begun in the last three years that some inner discipline could finally win, at least postpone the sense of asphyxiation. But its timing was never the same, or his illusion of it shifted. He could keep his mind clear of illusion most of the time except when he knew it was beginning; then he told himself it wouldn't come in the same way, or as rapidly, or it wouldn't be as severe. He detested the morphine as he had detested the removal of his freedom by slow degrees. He sighed and kept at the book which was about a man who had failed from a moment of cowardice in the Far East.

The Orient kept reminding him of spice routes out of China in the Middle Ages, the treks from Marga, Bactres, Khotan. How caught this man was, attempting a futile redemption in the jungles where a war had ended the summer before, caught by the tastes of French kings for spices over their carrion instead of salt, to make it less carrion, but carrion it was nonetheless; caught as he himself was caught spending a life at the edge of swamps in the state of Louisiana, a European man putting finish on his life by studying its failure, because dead kings and their nobles had a taste for caper and pepper and thyme.

The sea routes and the marking of the trades had landed him in this place as surely as it had landed that other fellow of whom the character Marlowe told unstintingly because dead men liked capered pig. It was complex enough—and all he had time for.

He had kept careful watch on the lawnmower outside the window but neither of the Negroes had returned to it. Its tongue cast a shadow like a sundial. The grass it had rolled over, pressing, had straightened again; St. Augustine grass, each blade like a long limp tooth. Perhaps today was the last cutting of the season; there was a smell of something, in the air, and true winter comes in an instant. He thought the jungles of which the author told must be like that grass exaggerated.

His son had seen the jungles, had spent the last year of the war in them. He looked at his watch: an hour until the mail came. Just as he thought the pain might be slower in coming, he thought his son might have written him so that today the letter would come. He didn't know why his son wouldn't write; there had been no words between them. He attributed it to the conflict of youth, but he had thought the war and the Pacific would have resolved it. He had written three letters which weren't returned. He'd only received a postcard in September saying the boy had been discharged and was going to school at Berkeley.

The failure of this man fascinated him, but there was finally nothing in the book to explain it. It lay elsewhere and had nothing to do with the spice tracks and the charting of the trades, or the place or time or moment, but its secret lay deep in the abbey, in the cloister of the intellect.

V O The town at night at the end of March, the winds having lain since the ides; red brick walls in the shadows, built since Wilson's war, not one more than two stories high; stretches of sidewalk with 1919 or 1926 carved in them, already growing old with time forgotten. There was nothing in the town that was truly recent, except for a fountain, a fox spitting water on that year, 1939.

He walked with a sense of the town absolute in his mind, its borders, its landmarks (one water tower which rose like a bullet on a derrick, painted black; one train track which came and went from the east to the west like the track of some animal that had walked over a corpse without sniffing or circling) and its possibilities.

He had been alone since September, over a year before; it was then she had left him. The agony since the twenties had ended when she went to put Webber through school in Waco. But Webber had not remained in Waco. He had gone to school in Dallas forty miles away, and she hadn't returned. Webber would come to Kemp on weekends to see him, perhaps once a month. It was Friday evening, and he had walked to the depot to meet the eight o'clock train which Webber might have taken, descending, smiling, a most handsome boy, most tender and quiet. They would have understood something about each other immediately that never changed, and walked off several feet apart, the distance narrowing as they went, finally talking, neither chasing the other with demands. He would have taken Webber to the drugstore which was still open then and himself fixed the boy a cherry phosphate and a ham sandwich and picked out magazines Webber liked to read with others Schilling had kept in the back in his office during the last month. But it had been only two weeks and he had gone to the depot on the chance that Webber would come for a part of the Easter vacation. He surmised he had gone to Waco.

Shadows of bushes, an empty lot, then the new highway (1936) that led to the same places as the railway, the lawns and his room in a white house two blocks from his office at the back of the drugstore. The flowers were fragrant and he hated to go in. He kept his car where he lived since most of his calls came at night, had always come at night, a grinding he accepted, and now with reliance on them though he was tired.

He had never accepted her leaving as no rational man will accept a failure of such investment. This part of his life, his marriage, was an arch he had tried to plaster into strength, watching it break. He had been relieved and frightened when she left; now he was both of these and isolated, the issues seeming remote much of the time, with currents of emptiness, despair, delight, terror and loneliness every tree and leg of furniture mingling with or evoking some hope or some memory or some irrelevant interpretation well-forgotten.

A moon was rising, an ivory spring moon above the black land and willows, houses, gravel streets, light posts. He walked a block past his room and reached the corner of the house where he had lived, a house he had owned for two years, someone in it reading the paper, bugs glancing against the screens. He walked through that block quickly, having no wish to be tempted by sentimentality, if sentimentality it was to find the experience painful. He wondered what Odysseus had thought of the waves on his returning, which must have been the same as the waves on his leaving. Going out he had something else to think of, of course; did he recognize them on returning, toward the end? Hope and surge of tides of going and coming, the art of life is intelligent memory, the dead in their essence without odors of their remains. Anna, dead three years; John, more than twenty. Who else? He had seen Eustacia Ardoin on a Dallas street three years before and had thought of her often but had never seen her again. To whoever thinks, life is strange and the fascination of recollection is a confrontation of human existence. Memory is man, and there's the game.

He turned left instead of going right where he was chary of walking through Negro quarters. It was the best part of town, a block of houses consistently imposing, a generation old or newer built with money the source of which puzzled him. The moon was on the water tower, its shape a pressure against reality, the tank wearing a hat this close, shaped like a Chinaman's. All of the houses had light in one room and he avoided looking into them. Odor of flowers and sound of insects, a lovely evening, and he had not chosen this evening to be sadder than others. He hurried up to get himself home, bathed, listen to the ten o'clock news, and asleep before the phone might ring and the operator put him through to some OB woman twenty miles out of town. He had three toward the Trinity bottom alone, and the river was still high, half the roads impassable except with mules.

He reached the corner and turned left crossing the street toward home when he saw through the window of a house whose owners he had never known a young man standing well inside the room, apparently in conversation. It was Webber.

THE TRAIN WAS LATE. For a long time he was alone, the track a dark whip laid out in its lines over the ties, a dream of a corridor vanishing. Cold in the dark though the month was March: no, now April. No sound but a dog's bark, and from far away a cock-crow for a false dawn. He thought of sleeping kings and the angels watching them in the French morning while cooks rehearsed across the fiefs. A cold morning, no matter where, a touch of history on the skin. He had left Joe in bed with his arms over his head like a sated sleeping woman. He had walked alone over the gravel streets, his feet as loud as wolves gnawing bones, past the rooming house where his father lay sleeping, no light in all of the town except along the main street and one hand light flashing on doorways, Knut Burns watching the town. Knut had seen Webber the afternoon before alight from a Chevrolet, the car driving on toward Mabank and Athens full of college kids. Knut would have thought it strange that Webber had dropped in on that neighborhood, his father living three blocks away toward town, if he had not become accustomed to seeing Webber coming and going without his father knowing it. He even knew about Joe. Knut, that fat cagey man who knew everything, walking silently in the night chewing a match, his hand light reflecting from a nickel-plated revolver. Knut had not yet come to the station to bring the mail. At two Knut had learned the train would be late and walked north past the doctor's room and had seen the light go on, the doctor on the phone. Knut had stood in the shadows of a lilac bush and watched the doctor take his bag and drive off east of town where the double-ess curves gave onto gravel roads toward the Trinity, or toward the black spurs, the black dry caked arroyos, called that where Knut was born in Eagle Pass, Texas, but dry creek beds here, made for flash floods, gullies crossed by wooden bridges under which tramps slept in hosts during those years of the depression, where, beyond some miles, wolves howled on some nights as late as World War I. He didn't like to see the doctor make calls there, and had gone with him often. When the car was gone, Knut went to the room and tried the door, found it open, walked in, found a hotplate that had not been turned off, poured himself a cup of coffee, using the doctor's cup, drank it without touching anything else in the room, rinsed it out, soaping it, and placed it where he had found it. (Only in this way would the doctor know Knut had been there.) Knut would sit in the darkness of the post office until he heard the train whistle and appear at the depot as the ground began to roar. In that instant Webber would cross the track before the impending eye of the engine and stand behind a shack until he could swing up into the locomotive and ride out into the weeds beyond the light Knut turned on at the depot. The engineer would grin and hand him a cup of coffee, slapping him on the shoulder. In two hours they would be in Dallas.

The train was late from Jacksonville, crossing east Texas bulging with Jacksonville tomatoes, almost from Louisiana, almost from the Sabine, through the Trinity country, bottom country split into willowy malarial farms with storm cellars and once-white shacks; sandy-land melons in summer and pines the train left sixty miles out where it made time once out of the hills, out of the true south, black and raging toward the Balcones Fault, across the savannas in which Dallas, Austin, San Antonio lie, black and lunging to the beginning of the west. He heard the whistle, that now dead haunting which the living remember who lay in untranquil sleep before it passed, remembering now when they waken turning in their sleep, swearing they have heard such a train again. Memory, skeleton of the past, its images ghosts, puffs of the dried dead, blown on updrafts from half-open tombs.

A vast snuffing into the road yard, the monster illuminated by its own breath. Then its tail, like the links of chains, suddenly slack. Webber pulled himself up into the cab.

Knut on time? Pringle said. (After Knut finished his coffee in the doctor's room, he walked past the house where he knew Webber was sleeping, and beyond to Negro quarters. There he walked in the black-mud chug road, the houses quiet, a moon rising late. He walked to the edge of town and looked over the dark land toward the wolf country, gullies and bridges lit by the rising moon, gravel roads shining, dogs barking beyond the grave-yard from farm to farm, yelping and answered. He loved the doctor, but he loved Webber too. While thinking Webber would grow out of it, he knew he could never tell the doctor anything that would hurt him.)

Yes sir, Webber said. I saw his light when you passed the coal yard.

Set down, son. He won't see you.

Webber sat on a tomato crate, a bit cold in the suede jacket.

Coffee good?

Yes sir.

How was she? Pringle snickered, his yellow teeth visible from a bulb burning over a pad and clipboard.

Webber grinned, very white teeth against a very yellow face in that light, a face the color of Costa Ricans, Spaniards or Italians. His hair was black, but it contained red that was caught in the light. His eyes caught the stoker's fire, their color like a Siamese cat's nose.

What is her name again?

Josie.

Good eh? Glad to help a young fella. Anybody see you this time?

No.

When did you come down?

Late yesterday.

When you get out of school for Easter?

Yesterday afternoon.

You going to Waco? Your mother'll want you down in Waco. She'll be looking for you down in Waco.

I'm going to stay in Dallas and study.

Well I hope your Daddy doesn't always think you shouldn't like Josie. Just a minute. Knut. Knut! We ready? About?—He can't see you—Near about?

A moment later the fireman swung up with a lard pail of honey, nodded to Webber, and disappeared into the coal car, In a moment Pringle used the throttle, the snuffing majesty moving unsmoothly forward, creeping toward the weeds; Webber caught a glimpse of Knut already remote, gone forever, irrelevant; then as though lost between distant places they clacked through the dark barbed acres, tower, town, shapes lost forever.

(Once, Knut remembered, Webber had taken the rim of a farmer's wagon wheel to the blacksmith, as a favor, the farmer struggling with a wagon load of kids and a mute wife, Webber offering to help the man, the wagon taking the parking places of muddy cars on a Saturday afternoon. Coming back, Webber had passed the jail, always empty, but on this day Webber had heard a cough from the one-cell stucco cube and looked through the bars, grinning the wormy-eyed tramp in the eye without a word. He went to Knut at the drugstore and lifted the city keys from behind the long nickel revolver, and still without a word, only grinning, left and freed the tramp giving him twenty-five cents, grinning at the tramp, and at the shot-rim farmer whom he met while returning the keys, grinning at Knut who hadn't moved, at the soda jerk behind the marble fountain, Knut saying nothing to the two people sitting beside him at the marble table when the keys fell on it. He knew what Webber had done. He thought of the Schillings when he walked over the town late at night, wishing he had the doctor's knowledge and his two sons and the doctor's gait, a strange gait for a heavy man. He found it usual that Webber didn't know that he knew that Webber was on that train already turned out in the night like a lamp.)

Kaufman's water tower reflected the spring red of the sun; a hobo dropped off in the Kaufman yards thinking it was Dallas, shivering in the morning. He stood lost in the early light. Behind him there came a man with a lantern, a brakeman named Lacey checking the cars for hotboxes. The hobo, half asleep, didn't hear Lacey until the brakeman struck a box with his foot, the hobo turning suddenly. Lacey looked at him, a gray-stubble man with matter in weak blue eyes.

Where you going? Lacey said.

Nowhere. The hobo said it flatly with no fight in him.

Lacey passed him by, kicking another box.

This is Kaufman, Lacey said. Moving on without looking back, Lacey said, You going to pick out west?

Yes sir.

This Is Kaufman, Lacey said, kicking another box, going on without looking back. The hobo stood in the pink sunlight shivering. It took him some time after Lacey had climbed over the coupling of two cars and was gone before the old man corrected his error, stunned and asleep, and climbed back into the freight car to crawl under the excelsior again.

The line moved, Lacey catching the locomotive.

Howdy, Webber, Lacey said. Webber grinned; he had been looking out the locomotive window when Lacey passed the hobo.

Lacey, Webber said in greeting.

Lacey said, Howdy Webber. Webber smiled this time.

Howdy Lacey, Webber said, Lacey sitting sipping coffee, the train rushing into the morning weeds, into the field of grass, alfalfa, high gear, planted young corn.

I'll get you to talk like a Texas boy yet, Lacey said, sipping the coffee, Webber grinning, Lacey giving a little grimace of his mouth, a tacit Texas smile. Webber read from a magazine, its cover gone. When they reached Segoville, Lacey swung down into the yards and when he swung up again he said, Howdy Webber, and Webber said, Howdy Lacey, and kept reading. It was a magazine in French a friend named Glen had brought Webber from Europe the summer before, telling Webber again and again of crossing both the ocean and the Mississippi, the crossing of the Mississippi of more fascination to Webber than all of the Atlantic. He had asked for the telling again and again, the river fascinating him, having seen it only once at New Orleans when he was ten, never having crossed it. He felt that the crossing of the Mississippi was more important to his life than the Atlantic: that first step of leaving for the east with no plans to return. At night he dreamed of the river.

When they reached Crandle, Lacey swung down into the yards but he didn't swing up again; the train pulled out, Webber at the window of the cab, passing him, Lacey saying, Howdy Webber; Webber saying, Howdy Lacey.

They crept through the outskirts of Dallas for twenty minutes and pulled into the terminal, Lacey on the ground when Webber alighted. Lacey started to crack his lips, then closed them. Webber said, Howdy Lacey, and walked toward the depot looking back, Lacey looking over his shoulder grinning with half of his mouth.

He skirted the Burlington Zephyr lying with diners waiting over their coffee for motion and distance, poised; he took the stairs into the depot and out through its marble into the bright light of morning, sitting for a moment beside the fishpool, its goldfish hunting quietly.

April in the pool, the fish swimming as bright as chestnuts, and what thought of heaven? Thirty days to the month, the sun bent over the morning as over a game. In the pool the cool fish swim brightly, the sun in their tails. Slow old men on benches let life skate by; pigeons walk past with a cocked eye. April in the pool, the light of April after a rain.

He heard the trains out of the woods, rusting, their sounds anvilling on the night, nights' stains in his mind's eye, sour iron in his brain's blood. He knew his father's curse, was cursed himself; yet he did not know how his father had endured it.

He knew the story of Eustacia from the time he had met Andrea standing in ballet skirts in a norther. Her thighs were pink from the cold; she seemed forlorn, standing in the wind along the wrong facade of the Medical Arts Building. He had reached around the corner of the building and pulled her out of the wind and tried to say charmingly that it was stupid to stand in the wind. He would have said nothing further, thinking that such dullness lacked charm, had she not, somewhat like a fox terrier, cocked her head, put her face in his, and said, I know which way the wind blows. I also know which way my mother comes from.

Then freeze.

He would have said nothing else had he not felt he knew her, a feeling that is never more than partially explained in a relationship. As though the whole thing had happened before, he saw the woman coming down the street, stopping to cross, then crossing, dressed in the same way as the year before when, in another norther, he and his father had met her at a Dallas corner. He had speculated then, and he knew that there was an island somewhere in his father's mind named Eustacia Ardoin MacIntyre, who had a daughter who danced. Seeing her crossing the street again, dressed as before, the strangeness of life descended over him.

He knew there was a story, and he pulled it bit by bit from Eustacia herself until at last he knew more than his father could possibly know. He knew that Eustacia had been released from the asylum at Alexandria because the doctors began, suddenly, to interpret her sickness differently, as though some new light had been thrown on the case. Eustacia only knew that Dr. Schilling had found some clear notion of who had killed Ardoin, and beneath the law, the procedure, the regimens of justice, Eustacia was released as cured two years and eleven months after the trial.

She talked of it freely, though yet with caution, and respect for the events, and Webber was fascinated. He laid his plans to talk to his father, but only when he, Webber, had his maturity in hand. Not before.

On this day in April, he was forgetting the dark nights of the past, coming out of his complexity. After meeting Andrea he came to know himself better, while before he had lived in nothing but puzzled and bent pain for as long as he could remember, nothing but contradictions.

He would hear trains off in the woods, in Mamou, Call, Kinder, Kemp. He wanted to go.

A day is a surf far out, a beginning of time, wrinkle of eternity, rolling, a sign, then color, light, long continuations, never to end. Then suddenly it is gone, the day, the surf, slipping back as though it had never been.

OFTEN HE HEARD THE TRAINS sounding evil in the night calling the soul to plunder, escaping in the distance, his soul going with them. Outside the window December rains fell, and he heard his father's feet on the floor leaving to go on a call. He heard his mother turn over, his father's feet fading, the sound of the screen door caught in the wind; the car starting. So cold, the rain so steadily falling. Hanno, Carthaginian, sailed down his coast past his fire-bright pygmy women, on plunder or contribution. A seaman died. The sailors gathered and someone whispered ancient history of that age: this is a dead man: stopped matter. And what, Hanno, did you say to that? So, too, the people of Punt lived beside a river in houses built on stilts. And Cosmos Indicopleustes said, the universe is a rectangular box with a transparent lid, a coffin. Suppose by chance there is nothing worth fighting for and when she first defeated him for her bed he thought he had lost too little for issue. Suppose having lived is no more than a mapping of where the mind has gone, lands of returns and everlasting regrets. One third of life is neither sleep nor work, but appalling loneliness. And this is the journey, the expedition into a world that lives only in one man, and can never touch another. The rest is forgotten, fall faintly thought before sleep or winter in still chestnut groves; or winter as cold cars and gruff births, grouchy infants pulled into existence, and long jaded streets in old country towns where one wandered while growing up, sawmill birds buzzing in the air even in the night, in the distance; wens on the mind. Sleep and work and the rest a chase, Socratic and doomed, Pythagorean and doomed, Jesuitical and doomed while the mind follows its path beneath the stars, among them, seeking to see them, at last to wander lonely as written language through time.

He had never won a battle with her. But wait: was he even on the field? Had he ever been on the fields of issue with anyone? How had he evaded it, how does he make himself so? How dare deny the bloodiness of issues and the corruption giving rise to them? To take refuge where? In belief? No, surely not in belief. Then how dare he give me this addiction to excellence and leave me alone? In my sleep to tamper with my blood and give me a craving, a second sleep; work, sleep, and a second sleep, this rocking of the mind. What set Hanno southward? Whom did he follow? Must we follow those who are dead to our under-standing always?

He learned the bones of the foot at eight, and the muscles of the body at ten.

Once they started across the Mississippi to New Orleans. They had taken a train on a foggy night and came at last to the river, slowing, bells ringing. The sound of ships passed in the distance; the train slowed, then moved over water.

Then he thought of his journey eastward, the train swaying in the fog. He thought of balustrades and empty armor, spears left on ramparts turned to dust with a moat between him and his vision, something that beckoned over water. At first a moat between him and ghostly arches, and at last it became a river lying to the east over which he must cross, with always a fear he would never get there. He knew only that he had to go.

For a time he was not sure they had come to a river. The train had pounded through the woods since dark and slowed for an hour and had crept as though there were something in the night to dread. Slowing more, there came a quiet, a sound of foghorns in the distance. At last it stopped and the gentle swaying began. His parents sat in opposing seats, her jaw set, his father looking into himself, and Webber could never break into either. He wanted to ask questions, the fog crawling about the windows. He turned white from the power of his dreams, thinking it was now, the mys-terious destination was near.

He turned to them, wanting someone to see him through it. He sat with his legs together, dark curls about his forehead, and tried painfully to think it through. Then he turned to the window and faced it, whatever it was. There was nothing but fog, and the reflected faces of half-sleeping people in the car. Beyond the window out of the fog tolled the train bell, slower than he had ever heard. He saw his father's face in the glass. His father touched him and felt him shivering, drew a coat around him, hesitated, laid it on his lap, understood, and said, We're on the Mississippi, son. The fog broke for an instant and he saw they were on a barge and he saw the water below. The fog closed again, and when it drew back, there was the river. Tales of ferrymen and music rose in his mind, trees on promontories, the river in silver briefly at the end of land, then fog for a moment, clearing again, the promontory gone, and there, the whole great river coming out of the north under the moonlight, dark and shining on the surface flowing toward them, in the distance as brilliant as fish, and alive. He could feel the water coming out of the land, out of bends of trees, a carpet sliding past, both promise and death, and as though there are shapes which minds take and swell to thought, he passed through all which later made his thought, that night on the Mississippi. He saw his father's reflection and began to feel the silence which became a part of him. He started to cry.

The water had not been rough, but suddenly he was thrown into his mother's lap, his father thrown over them. The jolt was enormous; his father fell against the seat and into the aisle. The lights flickered, pulses between blackness and dimness. People were shouting, The cars are loose. Some praying, some screaming, all in the time it took his father to raise himself from the floor. The car lurched again, harder than before, like an animal that has reached the end of its leash. People were bleeding, cuts on their faces; all were on the floor or half across seats. A woman ran down the aisle; the doctor, replacing his glasses which clung by one ear, grabbed her and pushed her into a seat. He turned to Quero and saw that she was all right, and to Webber who was picking his feet out of pine oil from an overturned spittoon, like a cat that has stepped in syrup. Webber began to comprehend the disarray as the lights came on full again. Perhaps twenty people were picking themselves up, and down the aisle a man was moving from chair to chair blindly, blood over his eyes and shirt. To this man Dr. Schilling moved first, caught him by the arm, made him sit down and take his hands from his eyes. The man kept trying to rub the blood out of his eyes. Does it burn a little? Dr. Schilling said. It's only salt. Put your hands down. The man submitted like a child. Webber climbed up with his feet on the arm of the chair and tugged at his father's medicine case in the overhead rack. It wouldn't come. He looked toward Quero and said, Mother..., and she started from her shock and lifted the bag down. Webber took it to his father who turned, saw him and said, Get the bandages in the bottom. In a moment he had the man's head wrapped in gauze, the man sitting with his hands in his lap. You'll have to wash your face with your handkerchief, Dr. Schilling said. The man looked up and said, I guess blood is salty, isn't it? Never thought of that. Tastes like it. He laughed weakly and moved toward the washroom, first in the wrong direction, then he turned and went the other way.

Two or three people came to his father and asked for bandages, which he gave with scissors and gauze, and they began bandaging themselves, helping each other, standing around the bandage and scissors. One man said he had jittery fingers, it would take a minute. Another said, What do you suppose we got into? A third said, Well it wasn't the Mississippi, you can thank your stars. The first one said, as he handed the bandage to someone else, This same thing happened about ten years ago. The cars just cut loose and we almost went in. Same identical thing.

A woman called to his father and Webber followed him up the aisle. Her husband was sitting on the floor, the woman frantic. Before his father spoke, Webber saw the arm himself, at an angle in which he had never seen an arm. Dr. Schilling took the man's handkerchief from his coat pocket and told the woman to get some water on it. While she was gone, he bent over the man, but Webber couldn't see. When she came back, Dr. Schilling wiped the man's forehead, then sat down in the seat and leaned forward and looked around the opposing chairs, at the floor, the wall, the window. His eyes lit on a pipe, behind it just enough space for a man's arm. Well, it's sure broken, Dr. Schilling said. Twice, above and below the elbow. And that's how it happened. He got it in behind there and snapped it twice. He thought a moment, looking at the pipe. I can't do anything right now but ease his pain. Would you get one of the men to help me get him up in the seat?

Outside the windows, lights were passing in the hands of trainmen. Webber heard their voices. Beyond, the river spread southward in the moonlight. He saw his father give the shot while down the car his mother sat beside a strange woman, the one who had been hysterical earlier. A passenger raised a window and said something to a passing trainman; Webber heard the word, doctor. The man with the broken arm smiled weakly and almost laughed and said, I caught at that pipe and she popped twice, maybe three times. I heard three times, I think. They started to pick him up into the seat; he looked at them oddly and said, I'm going out. His head went over just as Dr. Schilling said, Go ahead. Dr. Schilling felt his pulse a moment, then said, Now let's get him up while he's gone. They placed him in the seat, a pillow behind his back, then Dr.

GUILLORY

Schilling woke him with ammonia salts, feeling the pulse again.

Webber was the first to see the conductor hurrying down the aisle with his lantern still on. I understand you're a doctor, he said. A car's gone off. He whispered this, and Dr. Schilling's face looked puzzled for a moment, then turned white.

Going down the aisle they met another trainman coming toward them. There's a little girl in there with a broken neck, he said, speaking to the conductor.

Is she dead? Dr. Schilling asked.

She's got a broke neck, Mister; what do you think?

Is she dead? his father asked again.

The man saw the bag and said, You better look at her.

They went into the next car where the child lay on the floor. Webber had never seen such whiteness, with a tint of yellow. His father saw it but stooped, felt, then dropped the arm. He hesitated a moment, but took out the stethoscope and listened, then let it fall, to swing from his neck. Webber was squatting beside him. His father's face had tiny red veins near the surface, hundreds of them which made his face appear red at times, as now. He could see his father's jugular, and the beat near it which seemed to keep time with the stethoscope swinging slowly from his neck. His father was looking at something; Webber tried to sight down the line of vision. He was looking at the face. Webber then saw the little girl was his own age. When the stethoscope stopped swinging, his father leaned forward and touched her. He took her arm from under her and for a moment didn't seem to know what to do with it. He placed it at her waist, seemed about to clasp it, hesitated, then did so in a gesture it took years for Webber to place in his father's character; not out of sentiment, or affection, nothing as futile as that; but out of the decency of

88 –

farewell, and the kindred of man. Putting his hand under her head, the other under her knees, he lifted her onto the seat, then turned to the conductor and followed him to the end of the car. They heard the child's mother in the restroom with another woman talking to her.

Outside, the stars were as unmoved as sand. The fog covered the shore from which they had come. They were in the middle of the river, the current stiff and noisily breaking past them. At the end of the barge a group of men stood with several lanterns. In the center a man lay in a puddle of water, the lanterns shining on his face. Dr. Schilling looked at him then looked around the faces. Finally a man said, He was in the baggage car and he must have been drug down I don't know how many feet, and he come bobbin' up and Deke here grabbed him with a gaff pole, and I give him artificial what-you-call-it while they's trying to get them cars stopped. How deep you say the Mississippi is here, Mr. Beauchene?

I wouldn't try a guess on that; deep.

Well that's it, Doctor. And look at his ears here. Why is that?

The man's ears had been bleeding. His eardrums are broken from the pressure, Dr. Schilling said. He squatted to examine the man, and again hesitated to bring out the stethoscope, but brought it out anyway and listened. He stood up. Was he the only one in the baggage car?

Couple of animals, dog...and what was that thing?

Wildcat, going to the zoo in New Orleans, someone said.

The man who had seen the body float up looked into the water, stepped toward it; they all stepped toward it and looked deep into its black as though the baggage car were directly beneath them, as though it had happened right here, though the barge had drifted two miles down the river and the very water in which the splash was made was as disseminate and irrecoverable as time.

Cats sure don't like water, one man said as they all looked into the black river— trainmen, doctor and child.

ONE WINTRY DAY THE DOCTOR had waited for them by the pool. Webber had seen him first, pacing to keep warm, his hands gloved, the old overcoat thick in the shoulders, and blowing thin at the bottom. Webber swore he would replace that coat the moment he earned any money. But why was he there? They had taken the train to Dallas that morning, Webber, Quero, the boy Tom, and they were returning to the depot to wait three hours where it was warm. Why was he there? He saw them and stopped pacing and came toward them and halfway to them, turned back and stood by the pool. Webber crossed against the light and hurried toward him.

The pool was skimmed with ice, the fish deep in the grass.

Dad? Webber said. What's the matter?

Wait till your mother comes.

Webber waited, looking at the fish, quite afraid.

What is it, Dr. Schilling? she said, puffing. The child Tom hung back, also afraid; then he came up and stood between his mother and father; his father turned and faced her; Webber stood looking into the pool. He knew something about this, knew what it was before his father spoke.

Anna is dead, Dr. Schilling said.

Oh my Lord, how did it happen? Quero said.

Webber wondered what his father would say, and in the silence in which the doctor seemed to make up his mind, Webber followed his father's thoughts, confronted for the first time with the genuine issues which had always been a mystery to him. He had been looking through his father's desk a week before and had seen a receipt for two hundred and fifty dollars paid to a Dallas hospital for Anna Schilling. He knew his mother didn't know she had been in Dallas.

Well tell me, she said.

I kept her in the hospital here in Dallas. I didn't tell you because I thought it would worry you.

Webber listened to this lie and thought that he would have told it himself under the circumstances. Yet he wondered if it was the only way, and he didn't know. But his mother surprised him as she always did; there was never any way to know how she might behave.

She said, Well, you did the right thing, Tom.

He turned and looked at the pool, then turned toward her and said, Thank you, Quero.

You did the right thing, Quero said again when they had gotten in the car. Poor Anna. What was the matter?

She had cancer of the spine. I've kept her in the hospital here for three months, Quero.

You did the right thing. She didn't speak again until the car was on the outskirts of town; then she said, I must seem unreasonable to you at times. I wish I could ever explain myself to you, but I try and I always seem to get upset. But I try, Tom. I admire a man like you, and I don't know why I'm so hard with you, I don't know why.

That night the wind rose. Webber met Tom in the hallway sitting in his bathrobe on the top stair.

Why don't you go to bed? Webber said.

I want to hear the argument, Tom said.

No you don't, Webber said. Neither of us want to hear it.

What is it about now? Webber, I'm afraid.

Don't be afraid, little brother.

I'm not a little brother anymore. Look, I've got hair.

My God, you have. How old are you?

Eleven. What's it about this time?

I don't know. Why do you want to know?

I'm not stupid.

So you aren't. The boy had been reading books, with a dictionary, some of which Webber had not yet read. Tom had found several volumes pressed flat behind his father's medical books two years before, a dusty *Hunchback of Notre Dame*, dog-eared volumes of *The Iliad* and *Gulliver*, books which Webber had never known were there.

What do you want to go down there for? If you're not stupid.

I'm afraid they'll kill each other, he said.

Webber argued with this, but they went downstairs.

The wind shook the gutters, banging drain spouts. Webber and he sat behind the swinging door in the dining room. The voices came from the kitchen.

I can't go, Dr. Schilling said.

But you must go. She's your sister. You can't let strangers take her home in a wooden box in a baggage car.

I can't go. I have my practice, I can't leave it.

Why don't you listen to me?

I can't listen to you. I can't do the things you want me to do. I can't do things your way. I can't; I mustn't. Quero, I have three OB women and a heart patient I can't leave.

I don't understand you, Dr. Schilling.

No, you don't, and you always want me to do things with *your* understanding, and I must do them with mine. I've done all I can for Anna.

And why didn't you tell me....

Please don't go over that again. Quero, I must send her home by train. Dr. Schilling started toward the dining room but she rushed and grabbed his arm and struck and spewed for a minute while he defended his glasses. When she finished cursing and striking at him her eyes were glazed, gray and vicious and there was no reason in them.

When you get like this, Quero....

You're trying to say I'm crazy.... Don't you say it, don't you say it. You'd like to put me in an insane asylum, wouldn't you, so you could have all the money.

What money?

Wouldn't you? Wouldn't you? You can't do it! You cannot do it! I have friends, and they know, they know....

What money are you talking about? Do you know that I saved twenty-five thousand dollars and you left Louisiana and came to Waco, and you built a house and in three years you spent twenty-five thousand dollars and then some. What money? Do you know what I have in the bank at the moment? One hundred dollars. That's all. We're in a depression. That's all. Quero, for fifteen years you have not been right. Since you had typhoid, you have not been right.

She put her face in his, squinted her eyes and cocked her head, screwing it viciously before his face, and said, We'll see who gets all the money....

Quero, I'm sick. He had turned his back to her and leaned against the icebox, resting his forehead on his fingers.

I'll pay you back for the way you've treated me, she said.

How have I treated you? Quero, I'm sick.

My friends all know what you are, how you treat me.

Quero....

You drug us off where your kind are, so I wouldn't have any friends.

What kind is that?

Louisiana, the dirty French Cajuns, Kemp, with your dirty kind.

You married me in Louisiana for better or worse.

Your dirty dead sister, I'm glad she's dead! Her voice trembled now, reached a high pitch, like a preacher. I prayed for her death years ago to sweet Jesus; sweet Jesus, I said, kill that viper for turning the world against me, for talking behind my back, for making my husband hate me, kill her! Strike her dead! And he did!

You're crazy, Quero. Listen to me: I can lift the phone and put you away. You know that, don't you? I've never told you that, but you know it. You listen to me: you say one more word and I will put you away.

He had never talked like that before. Webber knew what Anna meant to him.

Control yourself and listen. She stood there but said nothing, her eyes seeming to say, there'll be another day.

He went to the sink and drew a glass of water. Would you like a glass of water? he asked. She didn't reply. He took a pill box from his vest pocket and put two white pills on his tongue and swallowed them.

What's that? she said.

My heart's gone bad. I can't work as hard as I did.

What's the matter with your old heart?

Webber could see his father wince. He squeezed Tom's arm, and Tom squeezed back viciously. I hate her, Tom whispered, I'll hate her till the day I die.

I have a leaky heart. It's bothered me a little for the last ten or twelve years, but now it's worse. You must help me or I may die.

Oh my Lord, you'll leave us alone without anything; oh my Lord.

I have another ten years of practice, if I'm lucky, if I can take care of myself. You must help me. You must understand, when I leave this house everyday, I mustn't always feel that all the money I make that day, when I'm paid, will be gone by the end of the week. Quero, we are not rich, we never have been, we never will be. When you married me you must have thought that, because I was a doctor, I would have a lot of money someday.

You could have.

No. I couldn't have, not what you want. I never became a doctor with thought of money; that isn't any way to make money. None of us ever wanted money, none of my brothers, or my father; we just didn't want it except enough to live and a little for the children. No, Quero; it's as simple as that.

You could have had it. You were invited to New Orleans and guaranteed only eight hours work a day at a fine clinic, ten thousand dollars a year at least, and you didn't go.

I didn't want to go. But that is over, and we aren't starting out, Quero; we're finishing up. Let dead issues lie. Help me.

You could leave us flat if you passed on now.

He turned from her and put the glass on the sink and locked the back door behind which the wind knocked forlornly.

They did not hate her always. There were moments of great tenderness between Webber and his mother, and Tom, much stronger and not as melancholy in his reflection, was capable of total rapport with her. Webber was ill the last month before graduating from high school, and his mother spent days tutoring him so that he graduated with a scholarship as valedictorian and it was she who waited for him at the end of the exercise, his father on a call. Again she might direct her wrath at Webber for hours, and Webber would cringe, his spirit shaken, while his brother Tom would manipulate her with a mastery that partook of genius: he would conduct her emotions after she had orchestrated them, and if she were in a wrath, he would make her cry; and if she were morose, he would make her laugh. Both had the feeling, Tom more than Webber, that she wrote her emotions, as a symphonist composes, slowly building. Tom changed her moods with elaborate stratagems, sheer lies and convincing acting. Once, during an argument, Webber saw Tom leave the house and looked out the window a moment later to see him by the picket fence. He was rolling up his trouser leg. Webber went out to him and found him with one leg resting on the top of a picket, the sharp wood just above his ankle. What are you doing? Webber asked. I've got to stop her, Tom said, and before Webber could protest, he raked a gash into his leg and started crying. She's getting worse. I'll have to cut my throat yet. Then he ran into the house crying at the top of his voice and in the attention he got, the argument vanished, while Webber stood there, aghast, and completely bewildered.

Most of his life he had been bewildered, and unlike his brother, unable to take action, Webber slowly learned to accept all of the confusions, and he drew closer to his father while, ironically, Tom drew closer to his mother, as an actor to his audience.

ON NIGHTS IN OLD MAMOU when it would snow, his father would go out into the unguarded dark, footfalls in snow descending through the yard, the loneliest sound in the world.

Once, when he could stand it no longer, Webber put his robe on and followed his father. Ten minutes had passed and the car hadn't gone out the driveway. Webber took a lamp with him, turned the wick high, and opened the screen door and looked out into the white dark. The car was still in the garage, his father's footprints leading to it. Webber stepped in them in his slippers. Halfway there, his father tried the car again. Nothing. The doctor saw the light coming and for a time couldn't recognize who it was. He had not expected Webber. He made no exclamation as the boy came with the light, in his bathrobe and slippers. The light caught shadows of the rafters, buggy wheels on them turning like ghosts brought back. His father looked tired and said wanly, She won't go.

Webber held the lamp high. His father's hands were gloveless on the steering wheel; he blew on them, Webber held forward the lamp chimney; his father cupped his hands over it, wringing them. Webber touched the car and drew back sharply from the cold.

Maybe we can put the lamp under the hood, his father said. Webber moved past stacked cordwood and managed to open the hood of the car before his father could get out. He held the chimney close to the motor.

Close your bathrobe, son, and you won't get cold. He did it.

I'm tired, Webber. Do you ever get tired?

Yes. Sometimes. No, I guess it's just sleepy.

Then suddenly he said to Webber, Do you want to be a doctor? He had never said such a thing before, during all of the calls Webber had gone on with him, nor, during any of Webber's life, had he made such an intimate remark except in joking, the kind of banter between fathers and sons before supper. Webber saw what it must be, that very clearly this was something both had been waiting for. He felt a shyness at first, a modesty that is most often felt between children and parents, as when the children walk into a bathroom and see their parents naked for the first time.

Yes, he said.

His father made no reply and Webber didn't look at him, but watched the wires to the sparkplugs dance against the other hood. He was shivering but managed to hide it. Ten minutes passed.

His father said, Well, there'll be better cars by then. He pressed the starter on the floorboard, it ground for a moment and turned over and coughed into life.

Now go in and get warm, get deep under the covers.

Webber didn't want him to go. There was something now; he thought it was a beginning; he didn't want it to pass.

When will you be back?

Before you're up. Now go in as I drive out.

Webber went, walking as the car drove backward, reaching the screen door and standing there as his father watched him go in, then drove out the driveway, the lights growing smaller against the garage, turning, and then gone.

It had seemed to be the beginning of something, but it wasn't enough. Webber wanted to be let in completely, felt he had lived on a parallel with his father and they had never really met.

One night in the summer after Wolf's barn burned Webber sat watching the eastern sky where no moon had yet risen. In the distance were clouds which by day were thunderheads, in the darkness parts of them torn away forming high strands. The moon rose full, the fireflies serenading each other with their lights, frogs and insects loud in the grass, the bushes, the cane. The light was on under the *porte-cochere*, where a young Negro was putting a new starter in the car; Webber could hear him curse quietly from time to time.

He was waiting to walk home with the Negro once the starter was in.

Suddenly he heard footsteps in the road running toward them. At first he wasn't sure, he thought they were going past the house, but they turned in across the grass and came up the drive. Webber stood up and went to the steps and saw a winded Negro boy coming out of the dark. The boy could say nothing at first; Webber went after his father and brought back a glass of water which the boy drank at once.

Mister Wolf done shot his self.

Dr. Schilling seemed about to ask a question, motioned to Webber sharply to go get his bag, turned toward the car and asked if it would run. Yassah, but it ain't finished; ain't no lights. They took it anyway, the half mile through the mustang grove to Wolf's driveway. He left the car running and Webber turned it off and followed him into the house where he turned into the study, stopped abruptly, and said, I can't imagine....

When he moved, Webber saw Wolf face down across his desk. He had fallen forward, half his brains exposed, in his hair and over the desk and floor. His father circled, looking where he was walking, and at the corpse. He put his bag in a chair by the desk and circled until he stopped behind Wolf. He reached forward to feel the wrist but pulled his hand back before touching it. He completed his circle and stood in front of Webber whom he did not notice. Webber was sweating and faint, his mind stopped like a still-life. His father reached down and picked up a piece of hair with bone attached to it and looked about for some place to put it. Without wit or premeditation he tried to fit it into the skull where it belonged. He took a piece of absorbent cotton from his bag and wiped the blood which still trickled. Then he stepped back and,

GUILLORY

looking over the floor, found another piece of bone and fitted it
into place. He looked about the floor again and found a hairless
piece of the man's flesh and fitted it, and began a canvass of the
floor, working like a sculptor hurrying for an exhibition. Webber's
thought returned and, awed, he watched his father bending,
picking up pieces of hair, bone and flesh, trying to fit them into
place. He was afraid to speak and could not had he had the
courage. His father got more cotton and looked around the room,
then moved to the desk and wiped matter from it, skirting a terrible amount of blood over the mahogany. The room was completely silent. He knelt and furiously wiped the chair, the floor at
the edge of the carpet, picking up pieces of flesh which he didn't
know what to do with. He wiped and cleaned until he was out of
breath and stood up sweating and looked around and saw Webber.
He turned back immediately and dropped the cotton into the
wastebasket, and from the other palm, the pieces of flesh. He
moved to the front of the desk, leaned with his palms upon it
looking at the dead man. He crossed one ankle behind another, his
left foot waggling slowly, nervously in the air. After long study,
with impatience he turned, seeming to dismiss the problem, and
said to Webber, See if the policeman is there.

Webber turned and standing beyond the door was a deputy
sheriff. He was a man in his thirties, portly and not intense about
the eyes. He looked at Webber, first with defense, then with compassion. He was about to say something, had taken two steps forward, when his jaw dropped and he took his cigarette from his
mouth. Webber turned and saw his father wiping matter from the
desk with cotton and alcohol, from the chair, its leather seat, from
the paperweight beside the pen set. He skirted the blood for a
moment, then wiped across it once and used the wastebasket, took

another piece of cotton, poured alcohol on it, then wiped in great and small swipes.

The deputy passed Webber and took some cotton and alcohol and began wiping. Dr. Schilling pointed to a place and made no other acknowledgment.

When most of it was done, he took off his glasses, wiped them with the remaining cotton, and said, while he closed his bag, Get your men.

He walked past Webber, turned toward him once, and walked out of the house.

On the steps the Negroes were waiting.

Where is Mrs. Wolf? Dr. Schilling asked.

She's in her room,

Who's with her?

Her sister.

He fumbled in his bag and drew out a box and said, Give her these to help her sleep. Call me if she can't.

But she say she want to see you, Doctor.

I'll see her in the morning. Webber....

They walked past the car, ignoring it, and took the road through the mustangs, his father walking rapidly, paying no attention to him. The clouds had moved toward the north, still breaking. The full moon had lost its yellow.

The legend was that Mrs. Wolf was insane, that Wolf had once had her committed. It was said that she flew into rages and had once set fire to the house, and many people said she had set fire to the barn. Wolf had come many times to talk to Dr. Schilling and they had sat in his father's office until late. Webber had never seen his father talk to anyone as long as he talked to Wolf, sometimes raising his voice, then lowering it again to its former calm. Webber had heard his father say, You cannot do that to your wife, Mr. Wolf.

They walked through the mustangs, his father slowing out of consideration and they walked together. It seemed late, the high moon; a breeze had risen. In the dark trees beginning to move in the deepening summer night Webber thought of asking his father, What is death? but he was sure that he knew what his father would say; and as he thought of the answer, the trees bent low and whispered yes, yes. He might ask the question, but with the certainty of one who begins to know another mind, he knew the answer, he knew the answer.

I don't know.

When he left the pool that April morning he had studied the themes of his life many times; he knew himself well for one not quite twenty-one. The trains still haunted him, excited his blood and memory, shuttled him down spur tracks in sawmill towns, sounds as slippery as soap, greasing the mind into deeper privacies; the river was there from childhood. The battlements were fading, the sense of the past was quieting, not as anchor, but as color; he had grown to interpret. Life moved toward epitaphs. He thought of his brother, that they must hie close to each other.

He had his music and his aspiration to medicine; his antic nature which lay beside sobriety. His mind was capable of great amounts of work, and, lacking his brother's capacity to leap, Webber built mute bridges.

He felt no guilt from the night before when he had gone to Kemp and not seen his father. It was a moment in growing up. He was essentially close to his father and he would always be. Someday they would talk.

He gave no thought to Joe, a rather weak person whose sexuality had ceased to be experimental; or sensual for that matter. He thought of Andrea whom he would marry. He thought of April.

He was at peace when he left the pool to spend that April day. He looked back once and imagined the pool skimmed with ice. He walked to his streetcar which delayed for him, and rode with the driver to the car barn near Fair Park where Andrea had danced. He kicked blown napkins through the gates beyond which the fairground buildings stood like towers of experiments with papier-mâché dead leaves from the last fall still along the walks. He crossed Dallas again by streetcar and found Andrea in bed where, jestfully, he impregnated her. That afternoon he gave in to temptation with one of her girl friends. By six he decided to walk to his dormitory which was empty for the Easter holidays. He opened a psychology book, read for a moment, closed it with a snap. He put a fresh light bulb in his lamp, sharpened his pencils, filled his pen with ink, straightened his notebook, looked at an inking of the brain he had drawn himself, read a chapter from a physiology book his father had given him with the name MacFarland marching across the fly leaf in nineteenth century gall, closed it gently, put it away, and began writing a letter to his father filled with serious thought, half-finished it, folded it and put it in his desk, and wrote a postcard, saying, I will come to Kemp in May. He pulled a feather from his pillow and blew it away. Putting on a sweater he pulled out the light, locked the room, walked past Andrea's house, darkened, with a sense that the day had long been gone, caught a car to town. He got off in front of the depot, passed the pool now under a full moon just beginning to rise, climbed the stairs into the great stone halls where the Negro intoned, Tee and Nnn Ooo, Segoville, Crandle, Kaufman, Kemp, Mabank, Athens,

Jacksonville.... He bought a ticket and walked down the Katy track, saw Lacey bending in the shadows checking the Kemp train, boarded the Katy for Waco. Ten minutes later he saw the Trinity under the train, thought of his father along that bottom forty miles away. Out of town the car dimmed and Webber walked back through the cars past college students, through the dark dining car and the Pullman onto the platform where the city was lapsing in the night, the horse atop the Magnolia building ceasing to turn in the distance, the train in the country, swelling the air and grasses, the wind leaping to his face. He leaned over the back gate watching the city recede and masturbated onto the ties, spitting joyously into the red light, his semen silver, reflecting for an instant as it spun, lost and left in the dust and dark.

Small roads down which turtles crawl lightly end at river bottoms, embankments treed by willows, mud horsed only by mules unridden in the coon night, cottonwoods possumed, loose dogs foxed, the mud river mooned. One breeze from the south over the Trinity country that first night of April nineteen thirty-nine; one Negro male infant named Wright; one thirty-year-old mother of thirteen sleeping; one surly field Negro father of twenty; one league to the crossing where the car lay in notches of mud ten feet from the river thirty deep fighting to the Texas Gulf; one wagon four-muled; one seat, one bed piled with planting corn.

He rode against the shining moon that followed, legs straight before him, his satchel rocking in his lap, his palms denting the canvas at his sides in unstable purchase based on shifting grain. One doctor, one satchel, one driver, one load of seed corn one night one year, the odor of mud fishy in his nostrils, odor of rain from the clouds in the east through which the moon was passing. The wheels rolled through gum, bells of halter rings touching, the croak of leather as though alive, the suck of hooves, a drawing forward, posture bent by some force that pulsed with mule steps, some pulsation almost unsensed so steady it became. What makes a night?

A Negro spurt of snuff juice, one drop caught on one breeze against one cheek, the old pulse of mule hide strained by music of muscles caught in time and trace, a memory of crawfish crawling last week in this same spot before the river had risen, crawling toward the pulp of an oyster waiting somewhere lying by southwind naked somewhere: the scream. The aching wheel gumrolling; the corn crawling under him; a few insects spinning by the spring moon.

Across the bridge on foot, the river tonguing splinters from the planks. Thinking of what? His semen pacing over lessons, snoring over dreams.

He heard the wagon turn and join the darkness in the willows below the levee. Opening the car door he turned before getting in and urinated a rut away making a lake with foam. *None of which he remembered.*

Driving under the following moon he thought of the names of towns: Mamou, Call, Kinder, Kosse, Opelousas, Merreyville, Breaux Bridge, Athens, Dallas, Kemp. *None of which he remembered.*

Foxes by rivers run in darling twilights, in rare twilights, in unhedging times by strung moons waiting in woods by willows made: by shallows wade the coon, by flood the mouse swept with bark and limb, belief drowned in marble river-face, granite death sea-bound falling east then southeast. Webber by foetus wrought by sperm inclined by night fulfilled by Friday chimed by Friday dead by weight by pulse by chance taken by Friday weighed by thought incurred by dream wrought by day inferred by foxes rivers run by rivers foxes run by thought think of final things by night-thought of final things by car by moon by night by now fox by river runs fox by river's run foxes by rivers run 0 God the fox a river runs.

Now think of final things, now think of duty and dust quietude and past, propound profound: by foxes rivers run by rivers foxes run.

Which he did not remember: all of which he did not remember: none of which he remembered. What makes a night?

Now: the town, the curve before not one but two the school not one but two the night one whole by which

Now: the call not two but one by which

Then began begin, no

O when?

When he had by rivers foxes ran run thinking of final things, yet not quite, only of sperm inclined

Yet not quite yet not quite

Cars by rivers run car by river's run

Now? O now?

No now, I say no Now

Now, I say no

Yet not quite, no not quite

Then, when?

Then, when he felt the pulse, touched his sperm's back blue by one o'clock by no lessons dozing, by no dreams snoring, he said by no fox taught which by no river ran

Get the doctor quick, he said.

Dr. Schilling! she said.

Get the doctor! he said

Dr. Schilling! she said.

In God's name get the doctor quick!

She ran

Foxes by no rivers run

She ran

In God's name get the doctor, he said

No fox by river ran

Don't you see, quiet by woods by rivers quiet yet not quite, even then oysters by bays enclawed, bays by tides entimed, by fortune timed, by sperm a foetus wrought, but not even then, don't you see, not even then: unclocked, time rocked, don't you see don't you see

Don't leave him, she said

And he never did that week

I won't, he said

And he didn't, yet one hour by Friday in the darling twilight of four before

I'm going to sleep, she said.

I'll be here, he said

Before four he watched his sperm heave from two by which no river foxes ran in the culprit dark yet at four not quite, not quite, he left for not quite fifteen minutes.

I went for coffee, he said

And he died, she said

There was nothing....

Was he hiccupping? she said.

No. He was quiet.

You're a doctor? You're a doctor?

Foxes quietly by rivers run.

I BROOK NO WORDS in this sorry moil. The squashy darkness of human pulp, the thread of alignments, the ligaments of lies,
one strung from another, box hidden in box in box, the needle of
time.... All are too much. I saw men as though opened by incision,
their hearts and entrails nestled intact, curled in supreme economy
of space, the liver caged by a comb of bones, the heart oystered
among lungs, the testicles ensacked in oval dormancy, captive, captive, captive sleeping thread emballed, their ducts closed, no gate
to immortality. Yet I hated the knife and never cut, only probed,
lanced, poking among corruption. How I hated the knife. What is
the authority? The unconscious? Knowledge? Reason?
Intelligence? Ignorance? Time? Event? Accident? Error? An oli-
garchy of all and error in mighty decision authored by every con-
ceivable force. I knew better at every turn; event was nothing, intelligence was nothing, the unconscious nothing, accident, ignorance,
knowledge, time *nothing*. Then trace error! There was none, none
to be traced. Not even among all of these? No. I did not like life.
It was inimical to my matter. A cocci in brass; a spirochete in stone.
It was not life at all; animation disturbs, but lends nothing. I liked
the portraits in perception, the serenity of an idyll held clamped by
millions of years, whatever sun, whatever world. What of collision?
What of it? Meteors, suns, worlds in which no bacillus barks
toward its bronze. Collision, yes, even in portraits inferred; balls of
phosphor will transgress the frames in which the instant is held,
collision yes, but not confusion. Not that unsubtle mobbing of
parts, mixing of entities beyond endurance: the unicorn, the cen-
taur, the mermaid. These are compounds unfound in a marvelous
world, blinders against manless air, insults to space, crimes against
geometry. Collision, yes, if only inferred, while molecules burrow
into one another. There is nothing trivial about the stars nor the

sightless burrowing of atoms. I have never seen triviality; I have only heard it or been told to imagine it while my mind wept over what it could not mend. I once performed a postmortem on an old lady who had rocked in a chair as far as she could go over the edge of the porch, dying of what? I opened her and found no bone broken, but her liver ruptured and thus she died spitting bile. I took out the liver to examine it: it was beautiful with its edges tapered as gently as the tail of a fish, like a manta ray in purple seas, gliding in time, a plane pressed by time and space. I laid it on the table beside her and was interrupted by a young woman whose breast milk I had pumped and cultured, the report on my desk. When I returned I closed the old woman and moved her from the table for the undertaker to roll away. Again a delay. I returned to spray the table with alcohol and the liver lay there. I did not recognize its place. In the woman, yes; its function, yes; its nest under the comb, yes; its secretions, yes. I did not recognize this deformity of matter, its relevance in this design of circling stone idling in the dark, seconds clamped by eons, stones touching leaving no bones nor light long to travel: clean clear metered end. I shall become nitrogen belched by worms, grass held by no bronze: my carbon will fly with the grasshopper, taunt the trout, paint the screen with grasshopper spit, boil through the bellies of infants fed from cows' milk, stain the diapers, become colloidal with Lysol, be distilled by rivers and return to the sea. There I will diffuse with dipnoans and silently thread their bowels and some two thousand years hence be taken inland by a squall to be breathed by Socratic men. I regret this nervous portraiture, this mixing of reality, impure, soiled by imaginations with motives; such minds lack merit or true hope. I believe it; the nekton and the plankton know it, why not I? They have never fought their diffusion into stages once by heaven, gods, and devils. What dignity there is in acceptance; what fraud in voices pretending to eternity while bored with a second. It is filthy! this traduction of matter, the lies told about it in petty hope. I would not entertain them; words are lies, lies hopes. I felt at home only in autumn when death surfaces in leaves. In autumn, held before you see it by some sense gained in late August, coming separate from intimations, in spite of the rhythmic hoax of hot moons and early suns, the croakers in the grass after dark. It is not the pause that matters, that is the accident of schedule and labor, wind and tide and sundry signs, the habits of birds, the depth of fish, the thirst of the cricket. The leaves know; their stems are choked with cork growing in the unstable rhythm of light. The chlorophyll is less, though in that moment it is not yet gone; already dying. Then the turning, the sudden bloom on the lake, the cold rock, the slick evening sidling into my joints. No autumn jarred them from delusion; they still inhabit vulgar spring. If you study the universe at all you suspect a galaxy heads for ours sun for sun, eye for eye, tooth for tooth. Autumn made me tranquil.

Each time it was as though I had not been there before, each instance in October a shock. Men bray toward their bronze.

I asked myself at each turn of vagrant interest, is this final, is this complete; is this all? Is this what I am? What place will I nourish, my bones contended over in coming battles, lying glutinous in the soil? Summer still ascends, autumn falls.

VI

O *The past is stored in a man's cells without the slightest necessity of sense. Lying now on this November day he had already studied his life to satiety, the ancient cities of consciousness* sanded by time and event, swept over by nomadic images, the million-cluttered hooves of the mind, dead faces met ascending stairs long ago, the delicate hand of a bell-ringer as subtle as a poet's; dead horses ridden to earth. Intellect stepped back; it hunted the ghosts, it sucked the marrow from dead bones; it ate the flesh of the past; it drank the gall; it chewed the testicles of time, tore the vagina of vanished life; it asserted the cheat of mortality in stupid anger spitting bile, while he lay dying. The history of the mind is composed of well-sanded anger, the dead cities lying over dead times of brute gnawing.

There was conscience, built not only out of sympathy—hungry Negroes, a Frenchman dead of tetanus, children scarred forever with sores from malnutrition—not entirely because of MacFarland, but out of a simple rational chemistry: things are better one way than another. He had had the intellect to say no. He had not accepted the sedatives of society. He had built a conscience out of solitude. He had found a way to live by his intellect with tacit images feeding it all of his life, the Negroes, the Frenchman, the children. The rest was private.

The mail had come bringing nothing. Sharply at noon, when the clock in the hall that had been built with chimes ground and shuffled without striking, he heard Mary going to the door for the postman, returning, passing his room. He knew then no letter had come, yet he called her; it was past time for his shot. He didn't want to ask, but he did.

Was that the postman?

Yes, Tom.

Nothing for me, eh?

No, Tom.

I'd better have my shot.

You get back into bed by yourself?

I ... think I sat up long enough.

You hurt?

You know I'm hard to get along with if I hurt very much.

She prepared the shot turning on the fire under the guinea boiler.

Where are the Negroes?

What Negroes?

Nothing....

Tessie's in the kitchen.

Boarders eating...?

Good many of them. Something in town today: luncheon or something for some war hero.

What you want me to do with this book, she asked.

Oh. leave it there, I want to look over it again.

Why didn't he write, Mary?

Fool kids, Tom; you know.

I guess so....

You're hurting...

I'm not going to complain today.

You could have had a shot an hour ago, she said. Let me turn that pillow.

Oh, here's my rice, he said. A Negro woman brought in his tray with rice, milk and toast. In the absence of gravy, he took his rice with sugar. Once he had cured himself of an ulcer by eating this same diet, but then there had been rare meat to go with it. But now his digestion was gone. He didn't want to eat then because the food in his stomach would crowd his heart which had already crowded his stomach to one third its size, and the dropsical fluid in his tissue, though drained two days before, was rapidly growing back. His feet were swelling, for a moment creating an illusion of health; two months ago he had weighed thirty pounds more. That was when he had taken the ambulance from Houston, from another brother's house where he had stayed, he knew beyond his welcome. He had been cow-

ardly then; the ambulance had been called a month before, and all the preparations made ready: he had gotten into the ambulance and begun to weep, the driver changing gears to begin the trip to Louisiana, and he couldn't go, he couldn't leave; he wept until they carried him back into the house where he lay for another month until September, the war over, and at once feeling the lines of the past, the map of his history in unheard of places; and even then he rode out of Houston along the oyster graveled highway called Telephone Road with no true interest in the sunrise. When the trees out of Orange told him he was in Louisiana again, not having returned except for someone's death since the twenties, he accepted the trip and refused to look back. Yet the war was over and times looked good.

VII.

It was the spring after the African invasion, when words like Tobruk and Tunis came over the radios, the war widening and drawing more into it, that Tom Schilling actually began leaving home forever. He would leave even before his father awakened, looking through the French doors at the sleeping man who had come home the last time during a February rain. There had been time enough since then for his mother to make a legend of how she had gone in a driving afternoon rain to bring him home after his second heart attack. Tom could see the rain pouring so thickly on the windshield it ceased to be rain but became immersion in continuous water, the air gone out of it, the highway a river; he could see his mother's agony, her eternal agony, hysteria, stopping beside the road for the rain to slacken, his father lying in the back-seat against the door, trying to quiet her, telling her not to get upset. He could see it without being told, and of how, with good intentions, she had intended, with mercy on her mind, to bring him home efficiently, forgivingly. Being there when his father arrived, Tom saw the doctor, a trifle slimmer, walk into the living room in his pajamas and sit on the divan, out of wind; he saw his mother go immediately to the room she had prepared and tell him his bed was ready.

Won't you come sit down, Quero? he asked.

I can't, I don't have time to sit down.

Just for a moment.

What for?

I feel I'm home, he said.

Well welcome home, Dr. Schilling, she said. And she sat down, her jaw nervously set, considering what she had to do next.

He didn't remember anything else said between them that afternoon and, in the two months since February, his father had become a fixture in the house, never leaving his room, scarcely his bed, though on some Saturday mornings Tom would see him sitting in a chair by the window.

He began leaving forever first by leaving earlier every morning, dawn on the doorsill, the lawn sown with jewels. Through March the winds whistled in the highlines, echoes of winter. By April the mornings were still, and he went hurriedly across the yard, leaving trails in the grass. In the last year at home he quit eating breakfast entirely and would take a bus on the highway across from his house to a cafe where he transferred. With half of the stolen hour he would eat hotcakes for breakfast and talk to the counter man about the war. A man who lived nearby who trained horses would come in and Tom and he would buy each other cups of coffee. The man never got to know Tom, but Tom liked him and admired his patience and expertness with the horse, an animal taught for show. On the bus that took him to town and school he had his first waking privacy of the day.

Most of his thoughts were of equal importance; he had lived inside his mind so much. They had no rank, no priority; he was equally interested in seashells, music and cars; movies, magazines and fishing; daydreaming, lying and joking. And other things bunched together about which he had found a lot of facts but no one to talk them over with. Had there been someone, these interests might have formed a hierarchy; but the people he knew wanted to tinker with cars, and he wanted to admire their beauty and love their performance. The magazines he had read ranged from *Captain Marvel* to the *Journal of the American Medical Association*, and anyone he knew was interested only in one end of the spectrum and not the other. He didn't think of music as a noise to dance by; he thought of it as something to listen to. He had hunted fossils where the seas had been along the Brazos; he loved a lie expertly told; he remembered every story he had ever heard.

One girl, the whole subject of sex and girls, travel, and books such as those by Victor Hugo and Joseph Conrad, interested him to such a burning degree that he was raw from them. Each day he gave a certain amount of time to each, and, daydreaming, traveled far away again and again. He wanted release and he found only suspension of tension in a movie, in a book, in the tiredness of weary frustration in the back seat of a car with most girls who were either wrong or too shelved in the south to give him either.

He was caught by time; he was too young to do anything he wanted, and when he became old enough he would have to go fight that damned war. The horror was that he felt he would never; a sense of irony frightened him more than the war; the war was only its agent.

He knew he was crawling out of the pit of their eternal agony, a blackness he remembered from the earliest, accepting it for years thinking it normal. Then he had no way of measuring the misery of either of them; he knew he had to crawl up if only to say life is not like this, though he had a fear it was. He had contempt for his father and a sluggish hatred; and his mother stunned him into both coldness and anger. He thought the whole matter indecent and that things weren't what they were supposed to be. But he had no insights into what was really wrong, and he knew neither of them.

He would wait for her at the head of the stairs with the second half of the stolen hour, in love with her so deeply that it became something to keep him alive, like the dreams, shells and books, and he would do nothing to disturb it. She would come up the stairs like majesty, her breasts bursting against her blouse to mock the mouth; she would climb the stairs like a workman hammering, or a queen going. Her hair was light ash, each wave as palpable as nipples. Her flowered dresses fell between her thighs like moving gardens, an arrowhead falling between her thighs. Her face was like peace and melons and the tones of oboes and ivory, her eyes the eyes of blonde young women whose thighs are locked to young men's dreams. She never knew why he was there.

On those afternoons during the last presence of his father he would draw his bicycle to the front of the porch content to say hello and then, leaving, beginning the going forever. Perhaps the beautiful one was to blame; she never left some level of his mind. There were eternal hints of vaginas everywhere—magazines, posters, postures—making him more private, experimental, masturbatory.

Then there was the matter of the currency.

When his father had walked into the house after the thunderstorm that day in 1942, he had carried an iron box under his arm, three inches thick, twelve long. It could have contained an ophthalmoscope except for the way he held it, not yet gaunt in his pajamas. Had there been any equality in that house or in any house where Schilling's children had lived, he could have asked and thus learned what was in it.

He helped his father sit down on the divan while his mother made the bed. His father said something, but he paid no attention to it. For years he had hated his father's weakness; this last was in character. He was curious about the box, and had he been able to ask, the matter would have ended.

Perhaps it wasn't the father he hated so much as the idea of a father; he didn't know. He knew how much he had tried to love his father regardless of her teaching. They had spent little time together, though after Webber's death his father had taught him to drive. Once his father had taken him hunting, and once fishing in the lake at Kemp, the waterboy calling the doctor to the phone at the pump house before the afternoon was half over. His earliest recollection with his father was a boat ride on the Sabine River in the days of Call or Merreyville to collect a fish for supper kept in traps at some point along the river. Perhaps because his father fell short of an ideal; but no, that couldn't be true; he hadn't learned the normalcy between parents until after Webber's death. When, out of loneliness for someone to be coming in at sundown, a shadow on a doorsill, he looked as far as he was allowed to run for someone alive, he began to see there had been something wrong; things were not as they should be. Before, he had taken it to be natural and whatever had been born in him from freshness and new life and whatever genes to which he was disposed, he taught himself to live in privacy as aberration. Out of this privacy his tolerance for eccentricity was born.

Yet his stunted hatred of his father wasn't because his father had let him down, or because his father appeared weak, but because of reasons locked into his own character for which he chose responsibility regardless of how they had risen. Beside his sensitivity, growing equally for a time, was an extreme brutality that now lay dormant like the coil of an undead snake. Young Schilling was amoral and only his intelligence fought it.

His tastes for life, a sense of beauty, a love of mental play, an allegiance built entirely out of sensuality ended the game and the last conflict where his monster truly had rights came during the matter of the currency.

Once the iron box appeared in a linen closet in the bathroom. Locked at first, he thought of taking the keys from his father's bedside table. He thought of prying it open with a fingernail file. Yet the next day he went to Montgomery Ward and studied the locks of all such boxes and came home to pick it with a bobby pin. After two such trips, picking locks for practice while the clerk waited on old women, he found there were three basic ways to open such locks.

It contained sixteen hundred dollars in fives, tens and twenties, mostly fives. He took twenty of them the first time, closed the box and returned it to the closet, opened it again as an afterthought and took another five-dollar bill which he spent during the next week. The twenty fives he carried in his wallet.

During the spring he was in love with her, one by one he put the fives back, each as a tribute to her. When summer came he went to Austin to college and by the following year he was through his sophomore courses and went into the army. By Christmas he was in the Pacific and there he began to piece together what had been happening while he drowsed by the pool of himself, riding the bicycle away in the afternoons across the lawn.

HE WATCHED THE BOY through the window riding in the spring light, the spokes of his bicycle in the sun, then gone beyond the gravel and the hedges. The only light in the room this time of day reflecting from the west, the trees of former tender leaves of early spring now rustling crisply, dusted, already dying as though they had passed their summer. Dusty since the last rain, as trees may become in August before the rains begin again. The trees in the shadow of the house were darkening. He looked for the flash of sunlight on the spokes returning, the boy maybe coming in to sit with him. Sometimes he came in for a moment or two. Schilling had thought to say something that might get the boy's interest, but it was impossible. It was impossible. He had tried, but each time with a sense that he didn't know who he was talking to. He picked up his book to read again, always expecting the spokes returning.

Tom had brought the book, Shirer's *Berlin Diary*. For three days he had read it, his precepts decomposing at the events of the chronicle. He could see the boy's intelligence at work, how it danced between possibilities and certain nihilism, casting back to thin coating over forgotten skeletons still dancing in the spirit of man; poised jaws of Tyrannosaurus Rex over the liver of Brontosaurus, all extinct because of a lack of taste, killing the wrong partners in their time. The fears and wisdoms so tautly shown in Germany of the thirties were as littered and sown as wild weeds, making no sense except as the geology of mind. Nazism and its possibilities seemed an insight into paleontology itself, idle remembrance taking form, as random as microbes or the fingers of the galaxy itself. Between the shots of morphine he had grown free of medicine at last: He no longer thought as a mechanic of thought, at last free for the first time. He had lost the faculty to see as he had been committed to see after MacFarland, a figure bent in effort over the quotidian, over blood and caustics, pus and dead dreams of immortality. He had known nothing when he practiced. Action obscured theory.

Perhaps it was the morphine that had given him abandon to formlessness, disinterest in human sensitivity. Yet urgency fought. Dope unloved him as his tricks of mind never could. Again it may have been total futility as though one were saying, *again*, it happens again. Isaiah, Ezekiel and Job—desert thought—have drawn the mind tight, all closed to freshness, time grease, stars bubbles in the gravy of man. The morphine wore off and the afternoon wore on and she would come, and whatever he had found dissolved in the knotting of motives, schemes, fears, lies, history. It was nearing the time for his shot, the sound of tires coming, no glint from spokes returning across the spring light.

THAT HEDGE NEEDS CUTTING, the car rolling into the garage silently, its bumper striking the back wall. Carrying the bag of groceries from the garage, locking it against the wind, pausing to admire the Hollyhock hidden behind the unfolded garage door. Tom was away, going she sensed into his adult agentry whatever that meant: to the war, whatever that meant; from whence whatever. She had seen him leaving, going...and she was lost. Help me: wilt thou be there in my dying? Will no man be there? Must I molt alone? In my grave beside nothing? No one standing above me

looking down at least in loss? Worded and by its complexity lost,
started and by dreams burned out, doomed and by duress
ascending because ascent was the name of man under duress
ascending. Dream of time passed, fatalities met, horrors, moments,
shams discovered. A branch had been broken by the door; she
twisted it off and carried it toward the house. Lilacs were at the
peak of their bloom, and the calla lilies were sappy above the
ground. Irises were in full bloom, violet, ivory and yellow flowers
she had chosen her first year here with a friend who, in ten years,
would lay such a purple quintessence across her coffin. (The friend
was the last memorable one who thought she understood Quero
perhaps because in Quero there was something honestly bitter.
The woman had seen this immediately and, bitter herself, instantly
invited Quero into her garden where she chose one each of the
colors that propagated. Quero had a profound capacity for grati-
tude and her loyalty to a friend capable of such a gesture could not
be unbound, however she might treat a friend; this particular
friend knew that, and the gesture of the violet iris laid across her
breast followed the separation of a year during which they never
spoke. But neither forgot the moment of the first irises when
Quero honestly needed and was befriended, a stranger in town
after so much failure.) The winter over, she passed the woodpile
without pause. Though gas had been piped into the house she still
kept a wood stove in the kitchen. She yearned for a fireplace; there
had been none since she had moved to Kemp for the two dark
years she could never forget. A wood fire consoled her, reminded
her of Papa and home from which she had never grown apart
except by the extenuation of fortune and marriage. This afternoon
she felt winded halfway between the garage and the house and sat
on a white lawn seat under a hackberry tree. The tree above her

was like an umbrella, yet when she had cut the seventeen hackberry trees in 1938, they had all said the trees will die. Before Webber had died, and he had said, They'll live, Mother, and he had died before they had come out fully the next spring. She had heard something of the war news in the grocery store. She hoped Tom would be able to finish college. But the war would surely continue for years and he would have to go. There was nothing else but him, now that Webber was gone. She was winded. Her legs, scarred from the disease of the thirties, were slim and bowed, their scars shining in the sunlight still on this side of the house, a silver-blue shiny flesh, spread along her shins; not even wartime hose could hide that shine. The rest of her was heavy, but not excessively for one of fifty-three. She had simply lost her shape; yet her face was still beautiful, without wrinkles, a grosser shape of face than youth had suggested; dignified and comely and human without airs. She felt her burdens too much for airs to suffice as a way through life; airs couldn't bear the burdens or reflect the joke, and most of it was a joke. This life, this betrayal. She saw verbenas, clumps of leaves, and thought of those growing around her son's grave which she had not visited for a month. She had had the stone cut and placed, engraved for all of them, the verbenas planted, the cedars at each corner of the lot, the grass mowed, the beds chipped of stray grass, the graves weeded; the roses she had pruned herself. As she had had this lawn of four lots plowed, harrowed, leveled, sown; the shrubbery pruned; the beds weeded; all done to its present state which, to her, was only a beginning. There was much yet to do. Since she had quit painting, landscape had taken the place of art. The woodpile had been her fancy; she had thought of painting it, but she had never solved the problem of composition. Now it lay depleted, its sticks awry, grass grown along its edges; nests of grass. Beneath the trees thirty feet from the back porch two wood lawn seats, once white and now rotting, bore the tubs where she did her washing; galvanized tubs upturned, the color of lead; the copper ribs of the scrub board torn, old and lackluster, leaned against a tree. The washlines were hung beyond, sagging between poles of scrap lumber that raised them when a washing was hung. The garage had been painted the year before, and three years before the house had been painted; both were white and fresh. Some lumber was left where the barn had been torn down, red planks split and stacked against, bent tin roofing damaged in the demolishment, slabs of galvanized roofing she hadn't been able to sell; she had thought of donating it to the scrap drive, but in back of her mind there was still, as always, the dream of rebuilding. Perhaps a garden house. For years at the house in the country she had set dimes aside and stored near-empty bags of concrete with only dregs in their boots. At every chance when she had a dollar she would pick up wire, and talk scrap men out of reinforcing rods. She got her sand by swapping a nursery owner four river cedars she had found along a creek in no-man's land. Then before beginning to build her arch, she consulted books in the library in Waco and sketched it to her taste dozens of times, sitting in the back bedroom of the only house she ever loved, soaking her legs in a solution of Epsom salts. Finally she had everything gathered and with Lucy's oldest boys to pour the forms and build the frame, she began her arch. She had it raised at one corner of the orchard where there was no driveway. Standing in the winds of March on her crutches she caught cold but ordered the work to go on until the rains began. Then the Negroes went to early picking and laying aside one crutch the first day, the other three days later, she troweled the cement onto the wire mesh, and with a ladder from mid-July, working two or three hours a day, she finished the arch in August. She had already decided how she could manage ten yards of gravel for the first of her driveway through her orchard but the arch cracked in September. She never looked at it again. Perhaps a garden house.... The brooder house had gone first, then the well house, the well rimmed-up with concrete fragments sledged from the brooder house floor. The barn should have gone first; no stock had been in it for three years before she had had Negro Ernest attack it with a crowbar, sledgehammer and puzzlement; neither of them had known where to begin. Finally he had borrowed a mule at her suggestion and tied ropes to six posts on one side of the aisle where cattle had walked to stalls for thirty years. Two mules were required for the other six posts, four-by-fours set by the weight of the loft onto concrete blocks. Yet it hadn't fallen. Finally Ernest drew a rope from its south door through its north and with a fourth mule and himself tripped it over, the barn lying noisily on its side like a great elephant dying with a whoosh of wind and disturbed pollen of fertilizer, an enormous cloud of time and crap and life. The crowbar, the pinchbar, the hammer and Ernest salvaged the barn plank by plank, the red paint coloring his hands, its dust flying into his face until at the end of the day he looked like a tired clown and she felt sorry for him and drove him home, the red on her car seats for more than a year. The well house was simpler, yet she didn't watch it. She had nothing to do with it. A part of it fell against the back porch and she didn't look up from her reading in the living room. She knew it would lead to giving up the well, and no matter how strongly she wanted to make this place into a habitable style, to make it a relevant home in which no one would ever live as though it were home, the well was the last of the past she forwent: those thousands of stoppings at wells in all light for water for thought, for talk, as strong in her past as thirst itself. The lawn was too big to mow. Tom had done that before he began to drift. Yet it must be mowed. She thought of her money for the week, how much she had spent, how much remained; how she would find enough for the lawn, to have the back screen fixed, the garage door straightened; the rain had caused it to settle and scrape. Now the rain was over, so let the garage go for now. There was more to do. Termites had attacked a rent house; a refrigerator had gone on the blink; a closet was scraping a hardwood floor. Sparrows were returning to the trees for the night. The leaves were again attacked by worms encased in beads growing wart-like along the leaf surfaces; a wind-injured limb from the spring equinox was dying and carrying with it a young limb. The winds terrified her. Not the northers that swept along the eaves of the house from October till March, as she lay in her bed alone, lulled to sleep by primal incessant howling; but the winds of September and colossal and rabid, tearing and ripping gales, gusts, cyclonic demons from the west, beyond compare; dying by morning, her terror white until the dawn, lightning still in the pulse of her eye. The essence of loneliness is found in a wind, gusting and dying like the respiration of horror itself. Malign. Horror. The gutters around the house were never the same after the wind of '40, and there had been no one to help her when two windows had blown out last winter; Tom was gone and his father was sick and helpless. She had used suitcases, jagged and worn from travels from nowhere to nowhere, holding them in the broken windows to keep the rain off the beds and floor and clothes, screaming until she caught herself and knew that no one would come. She swore against the fates as she ever had, cursing, screaming revenge against life, man, fate, wind, nothing coming out of her mouth open to the rain, her face and naked eyes wet in the prickling rain. The cat crossed the lawn, Tom's cat, its fur marbled shadows. She called the cat and the cat came and sat beside her, pawing her thigh as though nursing; she petted its head. At this time the milking would be done at Papa's, a wind in the pines, supper in the air. Someone would draw the last daylight water out of the well, and there would be no reflection until morning. How old I am. How old am I. I am how old. I am old. God, no. Death before age; yet she wanted to live forever, and she was afraid, of life, of death, of living, of tomorrow, of punctilio, of perfection, of failure, of duty, of the next moment, of dreams, of all and dust. The ties with money, the contests, the chicanery, the puppeteering of lives by spectral masters, a depression, a bad year; the chestnutting cat, the fool in the well: all are too much, and the four sisters failed. She rose and *sicced* the cat off her lap and started in. She wondered how different she might hope it could have been. She stopped to take linen off the line under the porch, holding the bag of groceries in one arm. Letting the cloth fall to her shoulder, she stepped to the well and looked down a hundred feet, the water dark with a faint reflection. She had studied wells all of her life, the deep eye holding a reflection of herself, like looking into time and unlived years around corners into promises. Her teeth were tight behind thinned lips; she looked with a cold eye. She stepped back and retrieved an apron she had dropped, reached for the screen door and went in. She now dreaded entering the kitchen since servants were impossible, not only because there was no money, but they were embroiled in the war. The kitchen was the last original part of the house. Elsewhere she had built new rooms, porches, decorated the old. The sink was littered with dishes. Above the table on shelves the china she had bought in 1920 bore oily dust; she had not used it since Webber died. On the table a silver vase bore two irises, the vase from her mother, the irises placed there to compensate for the duty she had neglected to perform. The crystal punchbowl bought in 1922 sat at one end of the drainboard holding boxes of keys, folded napkins, a padlock and hinge with nails protruding, a half dozen dead candles. A hammer and level rested in the dust atop a water heater. She sighed and passed into the dining room which for three years had been her bedroom, the dining set sold, buffet, china closet, chairs and table, after rain in the storeroom had warped the veneer. Only one of her paintings remained in this room, a sketch for a railroad vanishing. She removed the pin from her hat before the dresser and went immediately through the French doors, crossing the hall to his open door, the room darkening, the doctor lying still in the rapidly closing light.

ARE YOU AWAKE? He had heard the car drive in, and then thought he had been mistaken when she didn't appear at the door, her hair still auburn though she used rinse to hide the gray. He dreaded her, yet he wanted her to come, not only as something to look forward to, but as the root of a form that promised function, tonsil or vermiform appendix or enigmatic pineal gland. He still wanted what she had never been, and when he had come to live in her house this final time, he had hoped she would open like a flower late in blooming. Her house: all the houses had been her houses. He suffered to think again of the forces that propelled her. Had she always been this way? Enigmatic, contradictory, brutal and most tender, both dreamer and realist, beautiful and monstrous, vindictive and consummately understanding, sympathetic and repelled, her circuits untraceable. He could remember when she was only highstrung and young, the maniacal rages unthink-

G U I L L O R Y

able to her. His mind was dwarfed by the contrast: Mamou in 1906, a full yet trim young woman with long auburn hair opening the door to the boarding house which he later owned, standing, smiling before they had met one fall afternoon coming home with his grip in his hand, his gloves worn from the reins of the black trotter still hitched to the buggy; standing in the door in a lilac dress, the truest beauty he had seen since Louisville, trying to make herself small to allow him to pass, now as she stood in the door to the west, somewhat pathetic in her fifties, squabby, yet dignified and still beautiful. What had he thought on that autumn day? What had he expected? He was saved from thinking of it, and there was no need to.

He never knew how much love had been replaced by pity: for her illnesses, for her dead dreams, for her hot enraged vision. The change had come after she had had typhoid in 1924, from nursing him. He had never blamed himself for this coincidence; the blame, the answer, the fault lay deep in some cloister of his intellect.

There was no forewarning not only of what life held; there was no hint of the degree of disaster. He had been drawn to this moment inexorably, as he had been drawn to the presence of the retching and the sick, unable to turn for once.

I'm awake.

SHE WENT INTO THE ROOM where the light was colorless and formless. A glass of water on his bed table, now inaccurate in the shapeless light, held beads in its inner surface, the water stale, the glass warm. She looked at his sloughing form and put her hand to his forehead, telling him he had fallen asleep with his glasses on. She felt of his pulse, her toe tapping ten seconds. The pulse beat seven in that ten seconds. A blanket was rolled at his feet, a sheet covering him to chest. His pajamas were open, the hair of his chest black, graying, foreign to him she thought, like fungus. She had never accepted his hairiness. Her brothers were sparse-chested, men whose skins were white; this man's skin was more like leather; like Webber. Tom was like her, white and blue-veined with only a little hair, a man of straw color that diminished with maturity. She thought of him as English, Scotch and Welsh. Webber was the Frenchman, like his father, brooding, seductive, like a trap. Tom was volatile yet Celtic, the twilights differing, the difference between mood and brooding, one occasional, the other a temper, a way of life she could never undertake to understand. The man on the bed would awake from some occult study to a calm, an acceptance and inquiry she could never understand, the change without emotion. He was seldom upset, he could not be moved, he betrayed nothing of himself. Had he ever? Messing around.... Had he ever been a companion? He had none of her interests. To see him lying here, hirsute, futile, the very beat of his heart visible through his chest, the organ so enlarged his breast seemed to bear a large tumor; to see his strength so waning, his flesh disappearing as though melting, frustrated her: she felt pity and remorse, yet she saw going with him the last of her dreams. He was an impossible man, perhaps profound because he thought so steadily; she wondered always what was going on in that mind and she had never known anyone who knew. He had never had a friend since she had known him; he had never confided in any associate. Once there had almost been a friend, a mechanic, a common grease monkey who had appeared to become a friend. She had insisted he end the relationship. Afterward, when she was in calmer moments, she regretted having done so out of compassion for one so alone. Tom was what she was, instant laughter, instant tears, neither for long, running, running, running, lying between. She had lost Tom long before he drifted. Yet while he was a child he had seemed the only one. When the children started dying she thought there would come a time when one child would fulfill her life and that had been Webber; she had put her hope there and he had died that sudden dying of strep in remorseless stupor, the hiccups ceaseless for a week until that moment when, resting quietly, he lay still and his father left him. She no longer blamed him in her calmer moments; she had left Webber when she could stand it no longer, when she could no longer stay awake, when the hospital corridors were decked with flowers in the late night and no footfall sounded. Then Tom to whom her hopes were newly attached with consummate strength: she had lost him; he had strayed from her tutelage. When he had begun to drift, and she knew the reason was the sexual drifting of youth, he had understood her completely as Webber never had. Yet she missed Webber the most, perhaps because he was like his father, a new promise of one that had failed. All had talent and none had used it, not even she. She remembered only faintly the Pygmalion myth; strange to recall something so dimly that so formed her life, her thought in the very shape of her mind among the needles and threads of patchwork intellect half-sewn, its lack of finish the essence of madness. Tom was herself, a new promise of herself which must not fail, which would not fail, which must never never fail. This man lying in the darkness had sown these children, the two girls dead in Louisiana, the boy dead so suddenly life was rendered senseless; and Tom riding toward the war. Where? This man had sown them, lying here a hulk of spent time and form. He was looking at her; what was he thinking? He must be cold. She covered him in the twilight closing his pajamas, leaving him to button them in the dumb light of evening.

I'll get you some fresh water.

What was she thinking? She had stood over him, her lips drawn, her teeth clenching. He was afraid she was going to begin, but there was another cast in her eye tonight, one he had seen before but which her actions always denied: during all of the arguments, the lost sexuality, the moments of closeness, the moments of hysteria and insanity, the cast of tenderness would come again but it never became more than most impersonal actions of kindness or a compassion she had at times in the greatest quantity he had ever known. Tenderness for thought? Was that it? A flash of a fish in a moment of time. Remorse and tenderness for thought and nothing else; no survey of her true environment as though she had never lived. No conjecture about man, no long sailing at night in a memory trying to piece it all together, the enormous pain of coherent form leading out of nothing into nothing, no recognition of what a mind must weigh to afford dignity, no sense of injustice to be resolved into acceptance, the strength required to accept far greater than all protests and damned lies. She had stood there as a wife might stand over her afternoon lover, renewed for the moment, and the moment had passed. He thought of her again as a nurse and nothing more. There was nothing of the past he might bring up to make her a wife, an intimate with stories to tell. He watched her stand there, take his wrist and feel his pulse as he had taught her to save time, looking out the window; then he turned his head to look where she looked in the gathering dark where the sparrows were settling in the trees, and beyond, nothing of spokes in the road.

The pulse had no truth in it, saying nothing of the rising toothache in his chest. The closed mass of himself covered his bones, wet and waiting for relief. Then she took the pitcher to the kitchen. He listened to her footsteps as though going on a long journey, feeling as he had felt when steamers left from New Orleans, enchanted, yet alone and left. Her steps were like thought, leading him. The mind is the world, he thought again; accurate, or thought is sin. There was no spoke through the window; he heard nothing but leaves and birds. He had seen no stars from this room. He had seen no stars for a year. For more than a year. What is more than a year? Anything is more than a year. He felt the anxiety for morphine coming totally. Under a couch in a corner he saw the stained pigskin of his grip. In it was morphine. He had only once given himself a shot with unsterile gear and cold water, shaking the barrel of the syringe furiously to make it melt; a rising coming on his arm later from the unboiled gear. There it was, some light shining on the black leather. He didn't know whether she knew it was there in one of the vials wrapped in felt from which once strychnine had been stolen. Eustacia Ardoin. He couldn't think of her. It was too much; he had thought of her too often. He'd thought of MacFarland too often. He had thought of his grandfather too often and he knew he had become these at the sacrifice of not having followed easier men.

Amonophyline: he reached quickly for the bottle, frantic. He took two pills from the bottle of digitalis, swallowing them without water.

He took a deep breath to test his chest. Terrible. He closed his eyes, tears coming from them in pain. He heard her feet faintly: only moving from the refrigerator to the stove. He thought of eating with disgust. He thought of the qualities of an organism, restoring itself, struggling until it died. There was a chance, there was a chance. He heard her close the refrigerator door with the sound of ice dropping into glass. Now he heard her footsteps. She was coming; she was coming.

HER FEET HURT; she wanted to take off her shoes. She placed the pitcher on the table and poured a glass of fresh water, the ice musical. The room was so dark she couldn't see his face. He sipped the water; she turned on the lamp. He started to clean his glasses, fumbling. She took them. He started up in the bed; she replaced his pillow with impatient hands, beating it. It occurred to her in an instant that they were alone, that no one was in the darkening evening but the two of them, that they were compassionate friends having met forty years before. The moment passed. She could see his pain and her emotions brought tears.

I have a pot of water boiling.

SHE WAS GONE FOREVER: five minutes. She returned with soup, crackers, coffee and a boiler of water. She placed the tray in a chair; she went to the dresser, read the bottle in the palm of her hand, poured out two pills, returned to the chair, put her fingers in hot water without flinching, lifting the hypodermic, drawing water into the syringe, clearing it, raising it to the light, then found a healed puncture and shot the opium into his arm. In a minute he smiled; in three minutes he felt the pain retreating. She was above him, looking into his half-closed eyes. He wanted to sit up and eat the soup. The morphine said: assert. But not yet. The sparrows sounded very noisy, something unsettling them. Perhaps a breeze; sometimes a breeze would disturb the high branches, the sparrows waking. No cars on the highway. No spokes. He tasted the soup.

The soup tastes good, Quero.

WHERE'S TOM? Without waiting for an answer she looked over the room to see what needed to be done. She picked up the book from the floor, closed it and put it near him. She went to the window, paused to listen to the insects, lowered it for the night. Lowered the blinds at the other window. The day was gone. What had it been?

It's canned soup, she said aloud to herself.
It's very good.

I'll fix you some homemade soup tomorrow if I can.
It's very good. Tom rode off earlier.
You've been reading this all afternoon?
Some; it's a very good book.
Where did he go?
I never know. Well I have to go fix my supper. Do you need anything?
No no; thank you; thank you.
Then I'll go.
Quero....
Yes?
Nothing....
I'll go.

Thank God. He was rising, his chest opening like a kiss.

She went to the bathroom where pensively she sat, then up the hall passing his room, her duty done, wondering now when Tom would come. She opened the front door, the living room stifling from lack of talk, stepped out onto the porch where the day was faint. The highway was empty down which she would be carried in ten years past this house in some yet unnamed phase of the moon, the hearse as subtly passing as a firefly in August, an instant, then gone forever.

One night on Leyte Tom Schilling stood on a pier watching the sun set. He thought of the islands south of here and the last months of the war; he thought of the sea birds in harbors in the south, of his walking the beaches on sentry, the times he had kept his mind alive thinking of the girl for whom he had waited each morning before he went to college. By metaphors of melons he had remembered her while winds drove off the Pacific across inlets laid by the sea; by dreams of moist petals he had remembered her, smelled her on the trade winds and wondered where she was, in what wind, in what war. By winds dragging across the great currents of the world, she came to him, her thighs in the sand, opening in dunes in the sand. Wings of cinnabar from easterly winds, his mind raised life from sand, birds and the mocking line of the sea that led around the earth forever. At his feet blood went back to the sea. Some Cro-Magnon, Missourian for a time, reached here, and like history, found his equality of time and salt. Making the turns of sentry, archetype of intelligence, he looked south toward hills, untaken ground; west toward headlands; north to the Celebes, in the distance destroyer smoke, an oiler limping past toward port. Fires on mental slates rose like fountains, birds of the past flew by. He had thought of her to keep his sanity when the nights came quickly, when he could not think of going home: it made life too precious. But he lived.

Then he became a lieutenant and he stood here and fancied that along this water, along those beaches, history crawled back into the sea, a whipped monster waiting to haunt, seeming to look back with a bleeding eye, saying, I will have my day.

A few nights ago he had stood here on another pier, since bombed and strafed, looking out over the straits through which the war smoke passed, out over Cebu, and beyond, the Sulu Sea; fires lit in pineapple fields as though there were no war. He had received a letter from his mother that day, delayed more than a month. Her letters were trivial, but he read them over several times and he read the footnote his father wrote at the bottom, amused at the saying that no doctor can write legibly. Beneath his father's scrawl, she had added, You won't have to worry about the property any longer.

He had come here that night to find some place to be. The phrase brought back old disgusts which the war had replaced with others. For months he had done no thinking about his past except for the girl who, as fiction, was harmless. But the phrase puzzled him and brought back emotions the war had washed out of him.

All he had wanted was to be free, of the past, of the terms of his previous life, the failures and the issues.

He felt he had done that, gotten free. He had learned to see his past, to subdue it; yet he had not seen it all.

After Webber died the house was dark for months. The day of the funeral the spring rains began to fall, and at night he would waken and think he heard again his mother calling him as she had shortly after midnight April the first, wringing her hands and saying, I've called your father, and he won't get here, he won't get here....

What's the matter, mother?

Webber's sick....

Webber...? He had not known Webber was home. Tom had gone to bed at eight.

She said, He came home feverish and went to bed and when I looked in he didn't look right. He was in a coma. I called your father and he just won't get here and Webber has turned blue....

Blue...? He got his pants on immediately.

I gave him an alcohol rub and he's better.

But blue...?

The light was low in Webber's room. He raised it and saw his brother deep in the pillows, his head to one side. He felt his pulse, felt his forehead, felt the band of his pajamas, loosened them, opened the pajama top, touched the flesh and saw there was a blue tint, the skin cold. Webber hiccupped.

How much fever has he got? Tom asked.

I can't get that old thermometer to work.

He looked at her, reached for the thermometer, saw the mercury was separated. He shook it hard; it was still separated. He took it over to a table and holding it in his fingers struck his palm against the table sharply. It had gathered. He put it in Webber's mouth, but it was no use, it fell out. Then he put it under the armpit. The skin was blue, the breathing shallow and labored; he hiccupped regularly four times a minute. Tom had learned some medicine from Webber, but mostly from the atmosphere; he didn't give a hang about Webber's kind of medicine, bones of the feet. He cared only for why and how things worked.

How did he feel when he went to bed?

Tired and a little feverish.

Did he say his neck hurt?

No. His neck?

Tom removed the thermometer; it said 105. That can't be right, he thought. He looked at Webber's face; the mouth would slacken between hiccups.

Mother, get a spoon.

She handed him a spoon.

What did you give him?

I was going to give him a dose of calomel but I couldn't get it down him.

Tom shuddered.

He used the spoon as a tongue depressor to look into the throat. Where's the flashlight?

She went into another room to get it. Again he depressed the tongue; a hiccup stopped him. He was getting scared, not too sure of himself.

When he saw the throat he was really scared. He said nothing to his mother but asked her to get some cracked ice; while she was gone he sat on the foot of the bed. He tried to remember, hadn't his father given them typhoid and diphtheria shots every summer? Surely diphtheria. He looked in the throat again and wondered if he should try to clear out the mucus. No. Leave it alone.

When she came back with the cracked ice she wrapped it in a towel and put it on his head.

Tom said, Mother, I'm going to go see if Dr. Martin is at home.

Her jaw was set.

Dr. Martin lived three or four blocks away; Tom took his bicycle. When he got to the Martin house it was dark and he was told that Dr. Martin had gone on a call in Negro quarters and he set out again, Mrs. Martin shouting after him, Why didn't you telephone? Why didn't he? Because he had to do something. He could not find the house and saw no sign of Dr. Martin's car. A half an hour had passed.

When he returned home they were taking Webber out to the ambulance. His father was there, walking beside Webber; he got into the ambulance with him. Tom let his bicycle fall and moved into the light where his father could see him.

Dad...? Is it diphtheria?

His father looked at him with eyes that could be tender at strained times, and without condescension answered him adultly, and said, No, I don't think so. But you're close. Go in now. Come with your mother.

He watched the ambulance drive away.

The bad boy, the erratic boy, the versatile late visitor to his mother's forty-first year, just under the rope, a stranger in the minds of the three who knew him, even Webber; the dreamer, actor, liar, reporter of incredible imaginings at first, then manipulator of passions for his own survival; bright against convention, unorthodoxly bright, seeing at once the forgotten or hidden, calling that important and never once having anyone recognize what he had seen; seeing at once what he needed neither logic nor experience to sustain, and thus suspect, always, suspicion against which he would always rebel; finally learning after Webber's death that he would have to learn to see, to arrive at, to attain what he had once reached quickly, by backtracking through the same process of study others made, first to see as others saw and to follow their paths to at last arrive after the tortuous process back where he had been before; otherwise he would be alone forever.

That incredible week stayed with him. The hiccupping never stopped. In the corridor of the hospital, when it was quiet, it could be heard as far as the elevators. Easter lilies sat before the doors of rooms, scenting the halls with an odor he would never forget. Room 318 where his father sat that entire week through every night, rising every few minutes to look at him until at four Friday morning he had left for fifteen minutes because he could no longer keep awake. On Leyte, when Tom began to see, not merely by leap but by thought as well, simultaneously, he saw his father walking the corridor to keep awake. At five his mother had wakened him and said, Webber is gone. Never.

There were the legends. He had died of streptococcus infection of the throat which led to the bloodstream. When the war began sulfa was used on humans; the day he died, at a kennel a block away, it had been used on dogs for three years.

As a second-hand flashes in the corner of an eye, passing its gold hour hand, the week came back, the empty bed where he had lain, the stench of lilies, the coffin, the eulogies, the cold wax dummy inside, the rain after the funeral, the empty house, the sight of his father going back to Kemp, something forever lost, more than life which can generate actions of the mind to be dealt with forever, the agony of nature, the coldness of knowledge, the contumely of waiting.

He drew close to his mother because of nights when no one came in out of the rain at sundown, and slowly he ceased to hate her and backtracked from where he had been and learned to hate his father who came weekly, showed his helplessness, giving rise to the legend of his failure.

As though there had been no war the sun and clouds had sketched something that should last forever. The canvas over the straits needed only sea birds, but they too were gone and in a moment clouds, water, air became dark.

He had turned to walk away, and saw on another pier a number of jeeps converging. Feeling his sidearm he had hurried toward them, unbuttoning the holster. He was a lieutenant still at war and the war was still on.

The M.P.s poured out of their jeeps making a ring of excitement around a Filipino sitting among his fishing nets. Suddenly another jeep arrived driven by a Philippine scout; a lieutenant got out with an M.P. band on his arm. The M.P.s fell back for the lieutenant, their pistols drawn.

What's going on here? the lieutenant said.

Sir, this Philippine National has got a Japanese and German

flag on his boat.

Schilling saw a sail made of patched cloth spread over the prow of the boat, part of it khaki shirt, part a Japanese flag, the rest old sail. Across the rising sun was marked a swastika.

The lieutenant looked at it a moment, then looked around him and said, All right, all of you get back on patrol. Get outta here.

They went immediately, only the driver remaining. The lieutenant looked at the scared little fisherman, spoke to him, turned and saw Schilling. It was almost too dark to see rank. They saluted at about the same time.

Urb, the lieutenant said.

Schilling....

Did you see all this?

What did I see?

Urb waited. I don't know for sure, he said. Casidsid, find out.

They moved closer together. Urb's eyes were both efficient and humane. Odd, because Schilling had come to see efficiency as warlike, thrift the essence of the killer, accuracy the essence of the hunt. Urb's eyes were like the eyes dying in Americans across the world, or somewhere opening to morning. Yet his eyes lacked the shallowness of the German eye, hint of coldness and death in its iciness, sudden suspension of man in the name of a bright monster. The first impression passed, and Schilling saw the blue of successful mariners who went to sea with a sense of death, capable of hesitation and sadness. He liked Urb.

Just a minute, Urb said.

The light was gone; the jungle was the horizon. Urb came back. It's stupid, he said.

Schilling waited while Urb fastened his holster.

He doesn't know what he's drawn on that Jap flag. It's a right-handed swastika used in India for good luck; a male swastika. The Nazis used a female, left-handed.

Schilling laughed.

Urb said, Well, you see what I mean.

I see, Schilling said, fastening his holster.

Can I give you a lift? What do you do?

Graves Registration, Schilling said.

Urb stopped a moment, then said, You can have it.

In the lights of the jeep Urb was a very sharp soldier, extremely sharp. Schilling was impressed. The Philippine Scout stood beside the jeep and saluted when Schilling started to get into the back.

Wait a minute, Urb said.

Casidsid, take off and see that girl. But be on duty at three. You hear?

Yes sir, Casidsid said.

Understand?

Like a monkey, he said sharply, saluted and took off running.

What's this monkey business? Schilling asked while Urb backed the jeep.

A joke. No, it's really talk about after the war when I tell Casidsid he'll be back in his tree, nothing to fight for. Don't get me wrong. I'm not talking about race business. We talk about how all you need to live out here is a tree, like a monkey. See?

Schilling said, Well, it seems to me he could think of himself as a monkey a couple of times in that kind of discussion. He could think that you think of him as a monkey.

Going up the hill Urb turned and looked at him. You think so? he said. Well, there's going to be a lot of that kind of thing after the war. This country's going to have its independence as soon as the war's over. It's something to think about. How'd you get into

Graves Registration? Have you been in combat?

Up to last month, Schilling said. I think they gave me Graves Registration as a reward for killing people.

Hah! Urb said. Where'd you get that?

Not really. But my Captain called me in the other day and I found out why. He gave me a shot of whiskey; think of that. He told me, as a matter of fact, that I'm not going into combat again until the burying is done here.

When's that going to be? Urb asked.

He said by the next war.

Your Captain said that? Why'd they put you in Graves Registration?

He told me they had found on my record that my father was a doctor, and I had intended to be one; at least I had taken pre-med. He said somewhere in the army's mind there was a connection between the dying and the dead.

So they put you out burying...? Did you protest?

No. He asked me if I'd rather kill men or bury them, and I told him I didn't know.

Did you tell him that?

That's right.

Urb drove along in silence through jungle that had been cleared of Japs three weeks before. There was still fighting in the hills; sometimes a breeze would bring the sound of fire.

It's not so bad now. I've been promoted to records. But you got to see what it was like first...? With four enlisted men.

You've got it made. Do you know that? You've made it. He's right, it'll take years to bury these men. Do you like the coconut wine around here? I've got some.

Sure, Schilling said.

They drank very late and it was good to have someone to talk to. It seemed as though he had never talked to anyone, at home, in college, in the army; Urb was the first.

He got permission to move into Urb's quarters and one night after they had been drinking Schilling decided to find out if there was anything to the rumor about Urb that he had been kicked out of West Point. Just drunk enough to make a frontal attack.

Urb, why did you get kicked out of West Point?

Who says I did?

Urb, why did you get kicked out of West Point?

He waited a moment. My father was a Prussian kind of man though he was only part German, mostly Norwegian. He wanted to be a German, and he wanted me to be a German. I didn't know any better, so when I found out, I resigned.

When you found out...? You resigned?

In my last semester.

I don't know why you resigned, Urb.

When I found out what it meant to be a German, a Prussian. Understand that?

Go ahead.

My father was a very strong man, and that was his weakness.

It was a lie. You know? He was a very strong weak man, Schilling said.

No no; he was a very weak strong man.

What did I say?

You said he was a very strong weak man.

Did I say that? I'll, have to write that down. He wrote on the table with his finger.

I quit West Point because my father was a very weak strong man and I didn't want to be like him. That's all there is to it. The rest of it's a lie; I resigned. I'm going to bed.

Now wait a minute, just a minute. Let me write something down.

Urb went to bed while Tom managed to write the phrase down before he went to sleep at the table.

ON THE NIGHT HE STOOD THINKING back to the fisherman, the swastika, the first meeting with Urb, he had another letter from his mother. It said that his father had left to go live with his brother. His mind took its shape as stories which lay as tributaries, forming a course of events that led unalterably to a sea of troubles, a poor prophesy of life, a sad art, bent and homeless.

He had grown close to his mother after Webber died, and she had taught him to hate his father. On nights in that house when they were alone he had no image of his father; he lost all sense of where his father was, what he might be doing. Where his father had been, there was a blackness, a blindness, as though his father moved in black against black. He came closer to her out of loneliness and fear that he was like her. When his father came on weekends and the arguments began, Tom treated him, not coldly, but with eccentricity. He would leave when he had gotten his allowance, and when he came back his father would be sitting deep in his melancholy listening to her. Then he would leave and look at Tom with pain in his eyes when Tom wouldn't let his father kiss him, and made it clear that if sides were to be taken, Tom would take his mother's side. She had done her work well.

He would lie awake at night with unspeakable senses of his error; but he was caught. She had drilled him in what he was to say should he ever go into court to choose a parent. The only answer was to get away.

Once his father, while teaching him to drive on Sunday afternoons, asked how his mother treated him. He answered superficially, and hated his father for asking it.

Then he quit coming. He had taken charge of a small hospital in east Texas when the war had begun, and Dr. Schilling was the only doctor for half the county. Tom visited him a few times, but they spent little time together. On the bus back to Waco the dread of going back was mixed with quick inner joys and senses of beauty, a sunset over the prairies, thoughts of leaving. He shook himself and said to his body, Grow, grow; set me free.

He had not seen his father for several months when he found his mother's note one afternoon saying he had had a heart attack and she was going to him.

After a month of rest he got up and went back to work and a week later he collapsed and she brought him home in that spring rain.

Tom became aware of the locked door to his father's room or the afternoons before he would leave the house, the final spring he was at home. He would stand outside the door and his mother's voice would stop. Tom had stopped going into their presence when they were together. He would leave the house and not return until the lights were out.

Tonight at the harbor the fisherman's boat was gone, the smoke in the straits was somewhere else, north in the war. He had long ago made up his mind to never go home again. He would go anywhere as far from Texas as possible to become anything but a doctor. He had worked free. His foot touched a loose board in the pier; he treadled it to make it creak. He had worked free with some balance; his sanity had worried him since Webber's death. When he thought of either of them his hair stood up, the old burden coming back, all against which he had struggled pulling him back. He had made it. He was free.

It was the board creaking which like a feather slipping dropped the thought into his mind, complete, as it had always been though he had never seen it; and from the moment he saw it he knew, after the first horror, that he would never be free, that he would spend the rest of his life in some struggle for balance, that this was the nature of knowledge, to live cursed with reality, to live suddenly discovering what has been hidden, to walk a thin line between insanity and suicide, that this was the art and, somehow he had to acquire it and he had not yet begun. He had known it, it had been there, but it hadn't flown past the right moon to fall in place, drop the feather. The board on the pier had the same creak as a board outside his father's locked door when on those afternoons they were alone together until late at night. Then the letters about the property and his father having left. Of course. Twenty years later when he was still acquiring the art, he would say the words aloud as he said them aloud that night in Leyte, suddenly seeing how she had done it on those afternoons when he had dreamed by the pool of himself.

The morphine.

VIII

o *Late in the afternoon he awakened and found the day had darkened. He had gone to sleep after lunch; had he slept so long? He heard the clock grind and shuffle and threaten to chime. His watch said four o'clock. Why was the day so dark? There had been some reason, when he went to sleep, for calling Mary back. It was out of his mind now. The house was terribly still. For a moment he was frightened and he was breathing faster. The breathing slowed. Calm. Be calm.*

He lay for some time finding himself, wondering again how a man could come to this. He thought quickly of Eustacia but that time was so gone, so lost, and its meaning so unclear he resigned opening all the doors. He thought of the first time he had seen coal, a piece of it tied as a sinker at the end of a Negro's fishing pole; most amazing rock, compression of dead tissue that once held sway over the earth, and oil the blood of a dead age; it made no sense. He thought of Webber and how silent the hospital corridor was that morning. Easter Lilies set out before the doors of the patients, all of them asleep, none of them dying, even as they slept in fair health, in that most forlorn of all hours when it is coldest, lowest, just before some hint of day.

He glanced at the book of Conrad on the table; he still didn't know. He knew the failures of Lord Jim were not his; he had not been a selfish man. Perhaps there lay the answer; it might have been better if he had been. But that was impossible. Somehow there had fallen together a combination of a creature that could be this, and nothing more.

The most unbearable of all was the moment when someone knocked on the door of his brother's house in Houston when he was alone and he had told them to come in. There appeared in his door a deputy, Stetson still on, chewing tobacco insolently with yellow teeth.

You Doctah Thomas A. Schilling?

Yes....

Little paper for you. You bein' divorced, buddy.

She had promised! Oh those afternoons when she would come to his room and he knew it would begin he had nothing to hold onto but postponement of total indignity, total waste, total failure. Even when he could no longer bear the pain of the withheld morphine, he held out for her promise that she would never divorce him. That action laid waste to all the years he had stayed with her knowing her insanity was growing, made total failure of all he really valued in the name of person rather than in the name of duty or conscience toward the anonymously painful in his life, most of whom, of that thousand-headed moaning monster he never met as people. He relented and gave her the property asking that she leave him this.

There was still no sound in the house; but he thought he had heard something. He sat up to reach for the urinal, applied the duck-shaped porcelain to himself. Again contemplating himself he felt the pain of his smallness; she had cursed him early and he shuddered at the thought of coition. Suddenly he heard footsteps and he knew Mary was standing at the door. He tried to hide himself with his back and arms, conscious that his back was small. Let it go, it's too late now. No. He had pride; he couldn't accept humiliation. He didn't speak to her until he finished and lay back down.

Why is it so dark?

Norther coming.

I haven't seen Abe all day.

Abe went fishing.

Oh. Where are the two lawnmowers?

The what?

The two boys who were mowing the lawn this morning.

Haven't seen anybody. Didn't even know they were here.

Never mind.

You want your shot?

No. I'm all right.

I'm going to bring your supper.

What time is it?

Five o'clock.

My watch has stopped. She was gone.

After dark Abe came to the room, a fat man with a melodic wheeze, a fisherman by preference. John had been dead for thirty years. John had made the whole thing possible, Tom having quit school in the fifth grade to work in his father's store; John coming to him when he was twenty or so, saying, Tom, I want to send you to school. What do you want to be? I want to be a doctor. Then you go be a doctor. And he had gone. The night before John's death he had talked long distance to John's wife.

Tom, the doctor wants John to get up.

What?

That's what he says.

Why that can't be; he needs at least a week in bed. Tell him not to.

But he did, and by nightfall he was dead. Why hadn't the boy written? He feared he had nothing to show for his life and would not be remembered. Again he thought of death. And there was something he wanted to ask Mary. At that moment Abe entered the room.

You getting fat, Tom. Mary'll get you fat. Abe took the chair by the window, looked into the dark for a moment. Lawnmower out there; somebody'll run over it.

There were two boys here today to mow the yard: Pluyey and what's his name... Obadiah. Who cursed that poor man with that name?

That so?

They were going to mow, but there was some kind of business proposition; something buried in the yard. They never got back and I want to know what it was.

Well, I'll tell you, Abe said. Worms.

Worms?

Obie buried some worms in an old sunk bucket back a time, I saw them digging them up and we all went fishing.

Worms? Only worms?

Just worms.

Both of them began laughing at the same time. Why there's a lesson in that, Tom said. I thought it was going to be something, and after all, it's just worms.

Yes, Abe nodded, laughing, both of them laughing. Their laughter quieted after a time and Abe said, Getting dark earlier. Won't be long now.

What? he asked sharply, startled, frightened by the comment on his thought.

Cold weather....

He shivered. He thought of many cold rains, of mules at river crossings, muddy routes to farm houses, the terror the words O.B. sent through his bones at 3:00 a.m. on December mornings: cold black cars under his naked hands, wind in a yard light, the cars reluctant to start, their metal harsh: dark empty small-town streets that somehow lead to the rivers and the waiting jumpy papas, their mules dressed in mud. He felt for a moment the rain, the ghastly image of himself face up in the December mud too cold for worms.

Anna had died of cancer during the thirties, the year he saw Eustacia Ardoin on a Dallas street. There was something he wanted to ask Mary; was it about Anna? What would they have said if the horse had stayed out of the fence; he had never talked to her again in any serious way. Perhaps....

Mary appeared at the door.

Tom, I'm going to give you a little shot. Get you by till ten o'clock, then at ten I'm going to give you a big shot that'll get you by all night, at least till daylight. I don't like you getting up on the dark, no one to help you. Some of these mornings I'm going to come in and find you with a broke leg. The doctor said we ought to try this.

She had prepared the shot and he rolled his sleeve. She left to finish in the kitchen. Again he had forgotten to ask her something. He watched Abe dozing for a moment.

Did you catch any fish?

Abe was asleep.

He felt the morphine, rising, striking his coccyx like a tuning fork, floating upward, serenading his vertebrae sweetly, thrilling him, reaching his heart, forcing the chest to grow larger so there would be room for the heart. It reached his brain and he felt lifted into pure thought, absolute clarity and courage. How strange that when false facts are removed, the lesson learned from them remains. He remembered what he wanted to ask Mary, and while before it would have been rude to call her back, now it was the thing to do. Calling her name awakened Abe.

She came, having seen him like this before; she was prepared to placate him. She stood in the doorway while he propped himself up on the pillow.

How much money do I have left?

I don't know, Tom. The bankbook's in my secretary.

It's 6,830, isn't it?

I don't know; I got to go see.

Isn't it 6,800 some odd?

I don't know; I don't remember that.

Are you sure?

I'll go see.

Bring it here.

She returned and raised the lamp so she could see the teller's hand.

No.

How much?

5,380, she said.

He made no reply. After a moment of concentrating on a dark corner of the room he sat up in bed and dropped his feet to his slippers.

I've got to go to work. There won't be anything left.

He stood up.

Mary, send someone to see me. I can practice here.

He took a step, holding onto the bed.

I can put my clothes on and see people in the living room. You know people who need a doctor. I'll charge them less; I'll charge them a dollar.

He took a step toward the closet, holding onto the bed.

I'll charge half a dollar for a prescription. That isn't much. There isn't much work in diagnosing. I had the mind for it. It's a simple matter of thought. It's the babies that killed me. I told Quero I couldn't work so hard at obstetrics; I had to diagnose when I got older. I had to get a little money together and open my own office and take only certain cases when I got older. But I had to keep working for her and the boys. Webber died. I have to do something for the other boy. He's in the army; no, the war's over, he's in college somewhere.

He took another step.

I can see the mother but I can't deliver any more babies at three o'clock in the morning. You know somebody, Mary. Send them. I have a brain, isn't that enough?

Tom..., Mary said.

What am I doing? Mary? What was it? I've got to go to work.

Tom, come back to bed.

He reached the foot of the bed and moved toward her.

Mary, Mary, you're a woman. Don't you see, I don't have anything, I don't have anything.

Tom..., Abe said.

You lie down now, she said.

Can that be? Mary, can that be?

She put her arm around him.

Can that be?

You lie down now.

Let's do something about it tomorrow.

Yes.

Abe moved out of the room while she lowered the light and gave him another dose of morphine, the whole thing in the old way, making no changes now. She stood beside him until he was calm. When she left the wind was rising.

IN THE AMPLITUDE OF NIGHT the wind bellowed, horror to the cypress, dreadful to the bayou rat. Along the river Chafalaya girls lay by their lovers. The cabarets closed early. In the town a soldier got off the bus with duffel bags and headed home. The lights died in houses. The boarders snored and coughed, touched feet to the cold floor, urinated, pulled at the covers, breathed deeply of the darkness. The sheriff made his rounds; the train came through.

In the absolute night the bubbles formed again inside the glass, the curtains moved, the walls contracted. Shortly before five in the morning he gave himself a shot and lay back down. He relaxed totally, and died. In a few minutes the first boarder got up.

The man who lived across the street went out and started the school bus. Three workmen converged in the road and walked along talking. A tomcat crossed the lawn gingerly toward the house. Mary started the fires in the kitchen. A mop had frozen, hung on the clothesline in the back yard. A boarder reached out for the morning paper and the cat went in. The clock ground and shuffled and, as usual, failed to strike.

OTHER BOOKS BY PLEASURE BOAT STUDIO: A LITERARY PRESS

Rumours: A Memoir of a British POW in WWII, CHAS MAYHEAD
  ISBN 1-929355-06-8, $16.95, 201 PAGES, NONFICTION
The Immigrant's Table, MARY LOU SANELLI
  ISBN 1-929355-15-7, $13.95, POETRY
The Enduring Vision of Norman Mailer, BARRY H. LEEDS
  ISBN 1-929355-11-4, $18, LITERARY CRITICISM
Women in the Garden, MARY LOU SANELLI
  ISBN 1-929355-14-9, $13.95, POETRY
Pronoun Music, Richard Cohen
  ISBN1-929355-03-3, $16, SHORT STORIES
If You Were With Me Everything Would Be All Right, KEN HARVEY
  ISBN 1-929355-02-5, $16, SHORT STORIES
The 8th Day of the Week, Al Kessler
  ISBN 1-929355-00-9, $16, FICTION
Another Life, and Other Stories, EDWIN WEIHE
  ISBN 1-929355-011-7, $16, SHORT STORIES
Saying the Necessary, EDWARD HARKNESS
  ISBN 0-9651413-7-3 (HARD) $22; 0-9651413-9-X (PAPER), $14, POETRY
Nature Lovers, CHARLES POTTS
  ISBN 1-929355-04-1, $10, POETRY
In Memory of Hawks, & Other Stories from Alaska, IRVING WARNER
  ISBN 0-9651413-4-9, $15, 210 PAGES, FICTION
The Politics of My Heart, WILLIAM SLAUGHTER
  ISBN 0-9651413-0-6 , $12.95, 96 PAGES, POETRY
The Rape Poems, FRANCES DRISCOLL
  ISBN 0-9651413-1-4, $12.95, 88 PAGES, POETRY
When History Enters the House: Essays from Central Europe,
  MICHAELBLUMENTHAL ISBN 0-9651413-2-2, $15, 248 PAGES, NONFICTION
Setting Out: The Education of Li-li , TUNG NIEN, TRANSLATED FROM THE
  CHINESE BY MIKE O'CONNOR, ISBN 0-9651413-3-0, $15, 160 PAGES, FICTION

OUR CHAPBOOK SERIES:

No. 1: *The Handful of Seeds: Three and a Half Essays*, ANDREW SCHELLING
  ISBN 0-9651413-5-7, USA $7, 36 PAGES, NONFICTION
No. 2: *Original Sin*, MICHAEL DALEY ISBN 0-9651413-6-5, USA $8, 36 PAGES,
POETRY
No. 3: *Too Small to Hold You*, KATE REAVEY ISBN 1-929355-05-X, $8, POETRY
No. 4: *The Light on Our Faces: A Therapy Dialogue*, LEE MIRIAM WHITMAN-
  RAYMOND, ISBN 1-929355-12-2, $8, 36 PAGES, POETRY
No 5: *Eye*, WILLIAM BRIDGES, ISBN 1-929355-13-0, $8, 20 PAGES, POETRY
No.6: *The Work of Maria Rainer Rilke: Selected "New Poems" in Translation*,
  TRANSLATED BY ALICE DERRY, ISBN 1-929355-10-6, $10, 44 PAGES, POETRY

FROM OUR BACKLIST (IN LIMITED EDITIONS):

Desire, JODY ALIESAN
  ISBN 0-912887-11-7, $14, POETRY (AN EMPTY BOWL BOOK)

Dreams of the Hand, SUSAN GOLDWITZ
  ISBN 0-912887-12-5, $14, POETRY (AN EMPTY BOWL BOOK)

Lineage, MARY LOU SANELLI
  NO ISBN, $14 POETRY (AN EMPTY BOWL BOOK)

P'u Ming's Oxherding Tales, RED PINE
  NO ISBN, $10, TRANS FROM CHINESE WITH ILLUSTRATIONS, FICTION
  (AN EMPTY BOWL BOOK)

The Basin: Poems from a Chinese Province, MIKE O'CONNOR
  ISBN 0-912887-20-6, $10 / $20, POETRY (PAPER/ HARDBOUND) (AN
  EMPTY BOWL BOOK)

The Straits, MICHAEL DALEY
  ISBN 0-912887-04-4, $10, POETRY (AN EMPTY BOWL BOOK)

In Our Hearts and Minds: The Northwest and Central America,
  ED. MICHAEL DALEY ISBN 0-912887-18-4, $12, POETRY AND PROSE
  (AN EMPTY BOWL BOOK)

The Rainshadow, MIKE O'CONNOR
  NO ISBN, $16, POETRY (AN EMPTY BOWL BOOK)

Untold Stories, WILLIAM SLAUGHTER
  ISBN 1-91288724-9, $10/$20, POETRY (PAPER / HARDBOUND) (AN
  EMPTY BOWL BOOK)

In Blue Mountain Dusk, TIM MCNULTY
  ISBN 0-9651413-8-1, $12.95, POETRY (A BROKEN MOON BOOK)

ORDERS:
Most Pleasure Boat Studio books are available directly from PBS or through
any of the following:
SPD—Tel: 800-869-7553, Fax 510-524-0852
Partners/West—Tel: 425-227-8486, Fax: 425-204-2448
Baker & Taylor—Tel: 800-775-1100, Fax: 800-775-7480
Ingram—Tel: 615-793-5000, Fax: 615-287-5429
Amazon.com
Barnesandnoble.com

FOR PBS ORDERS:
Tel/Fax: 888-810-5308
Email: pleasboat@nyc.rr.com
Website: www.pbstudio.com

HOW WE GOT OUR NAME:
from *Pleasure Boat Studio*, an essay written by Ouyang Xiu, Song Dynasty poet, essayist, and scholar (January 25, 1043)

"If one is not anxious for profit, even at the risk of danger, or is not convicted of a crime and forced to embark; rather, if one has a favorable breeze and gentle seas and is able to rest comfortably on a pillow and mat, sailing several hundred miles in a single day, then is boat travel not enjoyable? Of course, I have no time for such diversions. But since 'pleasure boat' is the designation of boats used for such pastimes, I have now adopted it as the name of my studio. Is there anything wrong with that?"

- Translated by Ronald Egan

ABOUT THE AUTHOR: Terrell Guillory was born and reared beside the 98th meridian running through Texas, the dividing line between the South and the West, according to rainfall, farming to the east, ranching to the west—two cultures. He was exposed to other cultures as well: the Anglo-Celt and the German, the Mexican-American and the African-American of Central Texas. His parents' roots were in Louisiana, his mother from Winn Parish, his father from Evangeline, marinating him in two other cultures—Anglo-Saxon southern and Cajun French.

He was educated at the University of Texas in Austin and at the University of Washington, and he's taught English at the universities of Washing, Idaho, and Purdue. He currently writes a column for the Port Townsend Leader in the northwest corner of Washington state.

For many years he has divided his time between the Pacific Northwest and the Gulf Southwest. Most of his writings come from notes taken from glimpses through the window of a train which arrives too soon.